PROPERLY PUNISHED

MORGANNA WILLIAMS

Published by Stormy Night Publications and Design, LLC.
www.StormyNightPublications.com

Cover design by Korey Mae Johnson
www.koreymaejohnson.com

Images by Bigstock/Vector, 123RF/Raul Garcia Herrera, and
123RF/Konrad Bak

1st Print Edition. August 2016

ISBN-13: 978-1537138787

ISBN-10: 1537138782

DEDICATION

I dedicate this book to Kathleen Lowery, Heather Root, Ashley Thomas, and Sebrina Rose. Thank you for your continuous support and endless encouragement.

BOUND

I shivered as you secured my bonds—my arms stretched above my head and attached to the center of the headboard, with my legs stretched wide over my head and attached at each corner. I was spread wide, open for anything you wanted to do to me.

You smiled down at me, patting my cheek. "Okay?"

"Yes, sir." I was nervous but not really afraid. You would never hurt me.

"Good girl," you told me as you tied the blindfold over my eyes, the silken darkness surrounding me like a shroud.

My breathing suddenly seemed over loud in the dark silence of the room. I shivered when I felt a finger glide over the back of one thigh, leaving goosebumps in its wake.

"Did you touch yourself without permission this week?" you asked and my heart nearly stopped.

This was not a position I wanted to be in when you asked that question.

"Answer the question, little girl." Command was implicit in your voice.

"Yes, sir," I said quietly.

"Did you come?"

"Yes, sir." Honesty was my only option; you'd sense a

1

lie.

"How many times?" you asked as if only mildly curious but I knew better.

"I came five times without permission, sir," I told you guiltily, grateful in that moment for the silken mask that hid any disappointment I might see in your face.

Since I was tied in a spread-eagled diaper position, every bit of me was available to punish. I jumped and gasped when a sharp swat fell on my left bottom cheek. It was hard and left a biting sting behind. You had the thick wooden spatula in your hand, not my favorite by any means.

"Are you allowed to come or even touch what's mine without permission?" you asked as you began to deliver swat after swat to my vulnerable posterior.

"No, sir!" I wailed as the swats continued falling harder and faster with no discernible rhythm; somehow being blindfolded made it worse. It wasn't long before tears were trickling out from beneath the blindfold as the fire in my bottom grew.

I howled when you obviously turned the spatula in your hand so you could spank between my sore ass cheeks, each stroke falling on my tender anus and the sensitive area around it. You only gave me five, which was more than enough to get your point across.

"I'm sorry!" I sobbed.

"I bet you are," you told me. Then I felt the spatula pat the bare lips of my labia lightly and everything inside me clenched.

"What shall I do with this naughty little clit of yours?" you asked me as you slid the spatula over the area. I was so wet I could hear it moving over my flesh making slick sounds.

I knew what you expected me to say so I responded quickly, "Please spank my naughty clit."

The spatula slapped down without warning, catching both my labia lips in one swat. The burning sting was instant, then it snapped down five more times in quick succession. "Ooooh!"

Your fingers came to my burning nether lips and parted them, exposing the tender inside of my slit to your hungry gaze. The spatula snapped down again, this time right on my clit, filling it immediately with burning pain that quickly morphed to intense pleasure. The next swat sounded wet, embarrassing me but also making me want to beg for more. By the time the ninth swat fell, I was on the edge of an intense orgasm.

"Naughty girls don't get to come," you reminded me with a soft pat to the cheek and then I heard you walk away from the bed.

My clit felt swollen to three times its normal size as it throbbed with need. I wanted to cry again, the ache was so intense.

Little by little my breathing returned to normal and that's when I felt your tongue, gliding up from my asshole through my swollen lips and then centering on my clit. You licked all around it before catching it between your teeth gently so you could worry it with your tongue.

"Ooooh, yes! Please... oh, please..." I cried as you brought me to the brink once more.

Again you stopped just before I could go over the edge. "Nooooo!"

"Do naughty girls get to come?"

"No, sir," I wailed, my weeping core clenching repeatedly on nothing, it was so hungry to be filled. "I'll be a good girl! I promise!"

Again and again you brought me to the edge and then pulled back until I was weeping openly in my need as I begged you for relief. My belly was actually cramping, I needed to come so badly.

My head tossed restlessly on the bed that was drenched in my sweat. My whole body was one long sweet ache in its need to be filled, taken... given release.

Then I gasped as I felt the head of your cock stretching my sore slit as you pushed just inside my aching core. "Do you need my cock?"

"Yes, sir!" I cried hoarsely, almost desperate for you to fill me completely. In response you slammed inside me to the hilt, the head of your cock butting my cervix. The pleasure pain was welcome... needed... I reveled in the feel of you as you pounded in and out of me relentlessly.

The pleasure was so intense, I wailed and screamed as you drove me higher and higher until everything in me tensed and released in an orgasm so strong that I saw little white lights behind my eyes beneath my blindfold.

I called your name as I came, but I was so breathless, no sound escaped as my body tightened down as if to keep you inside me. You continued to move without pause, slamming in and out of me without mercy until one orgasm seemed to bleed into another and there was no separation, just unending pleasure.

When I felt the heat of your seed splashing against my inner walls I came yet again, milking your body dry as you pressed kisses into my neck. "There's my good girl," you whispered softly as you pulled free of my body and undid my bonds.

You crooned to me as you rubbed my sore shaky muscles and soothed me as my quaking body settled. When I was breathing normally again, you gathered me close, tight against you and I slept in perfect peace... free.

CONSUMED

Her heart beat fast, almost ringing in her ears as she lay staked to the ground. There was no malice in her parents leaving her here, they didn't have a choice; on the night of the blood moon, a pure sacrifice must be made for the good of her people.

The beast had to be given his due in order to satisfy his hunger and protect the village. This had been the way of things for longer than anyone could remember; stories of virgins given to the beast were as old as time.

Tyra had just never dreamed she would be the sacrifice.

When her name had been called, her mother and father had cried. But they still led her to the dirt altar high on the mountain and tied her to it. It was their duty to give up their child just as it was hers to satisfy the beast's appetite for tender virgin flesh.

Once she was secured, her mother leaned down and kissed her cheek. "Try not to be afraid, dear one. It will end quickly."

Her father had been unable to look at her, instead pulling his wife away to make the long journey back to their village. "Come, it will be night soon and we must be far away from this place."

Tyra cried silently as they left her; she was already dead in her father's mind and her mother was resigned to her fate.

She screamed, railing at the fates that had placed her here on this altar waiting to die. She didn't want to die... she was only twenty summers... she wanted to live!

Eventually she grew tired from screaming and struggling with her bonds and simply cried herself to sleep.

When she woke, the blood moon was high and Tyra felt someone watching her. "Who's there?" she asked fearfully, looking around but seeing nothing in the inky darkness that surrounded her.

A low chuckle was her only answer, the deep tones of it sending a shiver through her body. "Please answer me."

"Eager to meet our fate, are we?" The voice was deep and smooth, rolling across her skin in an invisible caress.

Tyra was mortified to feel wetness springing forth between her thighs from just the sound of the creature's voice. "Don't toy with me. Just have done with it, beast!"

Then he was beside her and Tyra's breath caught in her throat; he was beautiful. Tall and broad of shoulders and chest, thickly muscled and covered in a light smattering of hair; his cock stood out from his body. It was huge! Long and thick... a tiny drop of fluid leaking from the tip... she didn't really understand why the sight of it made her wetter and crave to taste him.

His dark eyes were piercing when they captured her own, seeming to see into the very core of her soul. She stiffened her spine and met his gaze straight on, refusing to show him fear. If he wanted to eat her, fine; she would not cower for him.

"You may call me Taruk," he said, a grin suddenly lighting his features. "Finally a sacrifice worthy of me. I've waited centuries; the ones that came before wept and passed out from fear before I ever touched them."

"You want me to call you by name before you eat me?" she asked with a frown.

"I'm not going to eat you, girl; well, not the way you

6

think… 'tis but a silly wives tale," he told her with another low chuckle. "I will consume you, make no mistake… I will have everything of you. Everything you are… everything you will be… your dreams… your nightmares… all will be mine."

"I don't understand," Tyra whispered softly, suddenly more afraid than when her parents first staked her out on this mountain.

"Blood moon after blood moon, your people have brought me virgins, but never were they worthy. I freed them all. I took them down the other side of the mountain and forbid them to return and gave them each enough gold to live well," he explained.

"So you are letting me go?" she asked, relief and joy lighting her features.

"No. You are the one I've waited for… my bride… you, my dear one, will never escape me… you I will devour… consume until your heart beats for me alone and your body longs for my touch."

"What? No!" Tyra cried as she began once again to tear at her restraints.

He laughed. "Struggle is futile, my pretty one. Your body already recognizes me as your mate. Feel how it prepares the way for my rod?"

Her eyes widened as she shook her head to deny what he was saying, embarrassed by the flood of moisture between her thighs.

Taruk shook his head and clicked his tongue as if shaming her. "Already lying to me, pretty one. You will have to be punished."

He ran one long finger up the inside of her spread legs and through the slick moisture leaking from her core; she groaned as he coated his hand in it before holding it up to the light of the blood moon so she could see it glistening.

"See how your body already weeps for me? You beg for my possession and you don't even know it."

She watched as he licked the evidence of her arousal

7

from his fingers one by one as if relishing the taste of her. Her clit began to throb with need as she watched the evocative sight.

"Mmmmm, a sweeter ambrosia there never was... I must have more," he said before using sharp nails to cut the ropes binding her ankles. Her arms still bound above her head, Tyra gasped as he suddenly spread her wide with her legs over his shoulders.

Then he fell on her, his tongue spearing deep inside her as he licked her as if he would indeed consume her flesh. Tyra could only pant and mewl in pleasure as he feasted on her slick heat. His tongue began to worry her swollen clit as he sent two fingers into her pulsing sheath, pumping them in and out of her relentlessly until she came with a scream, calling his name like a prayer.

Then his body slid up hers, his hair-roughened skin teasing her nipples as he kissed her deeply and the thick head of his cock found her needy core and began thrusting inside her tight virgin body.

Tyra's back bowed and she whimpered as her tight inner muscles were stretched beyond capacity around his girth. She felt impossibly full and still he moved, bringing more and more of him inside with every thrust.

She was caught in a world between pleasure and pain as her inner muscles stretched to accommodate him. Finally he was inside her to the hilt, his balls flush against the entrance of her body, and surprisingly she found she wanted more. "Please..." Tyra cried.

Taruk gave a triumphant cry and pulled almost completely out of her before driving back inside hard and fast. "That's it, little bride, you will take all of me and beg for more."

True to his word as he pounded relentlessly in and out of her wet heat, Tyra begged and pleaded that he take her even harder and faster, completely consumed by him and the need he'd awakened within her. With his final lunge slamming into her cervix she came hard, a soundless scream on her lips as his seed splashed deep inside her, coating the mouth of her womb.

Taruk pulled free from her spent body then sliced through the bonds on her wrists and picked her up. "Rest on the journey home, my love. You will need it."

Tyra was too tired from the events of the day to take in what he was saying and fell asleep quickly with her head resting on his shoulder, the rhythm of his steps soothing her.

• • • • • • •

"We are home, bride," Taruk said, setting her on her feet at the mouth of a large cave.

"My name is Tyra, why have you not asked?" she questioned him curiously.

"Among my kind a name is sacred; it is rude to ask. A name must be freely given because of the power it wields," he explained.

She frowned up at him. "My name holds no power."

"Oh, but it does, little Tyra, it does. Now that you have gifted me with your name, I will use it to bind you even more completely to me. I told you… you will never escape me," Taruk said warningly.

Tyra thought of the pleasure the beast had already visited upon her body and realized she wasn't as frightened as she should be by the thought of spending the rest of her days with him. "What are you?"

Taruk smiled. "I'm a shapeshifter; my people tend to live solitary existences. We long only for the company of a destined mate. When I settled here, one of the village elders saw me change and begged mercy for his village. I never intended harm to the villagers but I take what chances fate throws my way and accepted his eager offer of virgin sacrifices on the nights of blood moons. It was a wasted effort until you."

She smiled at him.

"Now we must see to your punishment, and then I will finish claiming my prize," he told her.

"Punishment?" Tyra asked in alarm.

"Yes, you lied to me, little mate... you tried to pretend your body was unaffected by my presence. There will never be lies between us. Then I will finish staking my claim. I will leave my seed in every orifice of your body, marking you as mine... ensuring you know who you belong to... who owns you from this night forward."

Before she could protest further, he caught her arm in his hand and went to one knee, pulling her face down across his thigh. His palm began to fall hard and fast immediately.

Tyra jerked in surprise. This was no child's punishment... this hurt badly. Her bottom began to fill with an almost unbearable stinging heat as his hand continued to fall relentlessly, until she was sagging over his knee and crying like a little girl.

Then he stood, marched her into his cave, and stood her against the wall, facing it. "Now you will stand here and reflect about the folly of lying to your husband."

She sniffled miserably as she stood there, her bottom throbbing from the most thorough spanking she'd received in her lifetime. She longed to rub away the sting but had a feeling that would only garner additional punishment.

"Come to me, Tyra," he called.

Tyra turned to find him standing a few feet away from her with two large pillows at his feet; she wiped the tears from her cheeks. "Yes, sir."

Taruk smiled. "Good girl. Will you make the error of lying to me again?"

"No, sir," she promised fervently.

"Good, lesson learned then. Come and kneel before me. I wish you to suck my cock." He held a hand out to her.

Tyra quickly came and took his hand as she knelt at his feet on the pillows, suddenly eager for the taste and feel of him in her mouth.

She caught him in her hand and brought the wide head

of his phallus to her lips, licking lightly all around the head at first.

He tasted salty with a little tang, but she found him delicious and each taste only made her crave more of him.

"That's it, Tyra, take me inside," he instructed with a groan.

She didn't hesitate to do as he asked, sucking him inside the hot cavern of her mouth as deeply as she could, nursing on his cock and licking it at the same time. Soon he was pumping gently in and out while using his hold on her head to guide her. She gagged a little but swallowed eagerly when he shot his seed down her throat.

"That's my good girl, take it all," Taruk told her as he continued to thrust in and out of her mouth as she cleaned his seed from his still hard cock.

He lifted her to stand in front of him again, taking her mouth in a thorough kiss as he thrust a finger inside her while his thumb played across her clit. He pulled his mouth away from her. "Wet for me again already?"

"Yes, sir," Tyra said with a smile; sucking his cock had made her need him again.

"Ride my hand," Taruk instructed.

She groaned as two more fingers joined the first and she began to grind up and down on his fingers hard as he worked her clit mercilessly. She held tight to his shoulders as she threw her head back, becoming lost in the pleasure of his touch. Soon he was no longer content to let her ride his fingers at her own speed and began slamming them in and out of her, almost lifting her off her feet until she shuddered and cried out her release.

Taruk wasted no time bending her across their bed and slamming his hard cock into her to the hilt before he eased it back out of her and spread her tender ass cheeks open.

Her eyes sprang wide at the feel of the broad head of his cock pressing into her most private hole for entrance, but found she wanted him there. She wanted to feel him everywhere, to know she belonged to him every time she moved tomorrow.

She pressed back against him as he thrust forward, groaning as her tender little hole opened for him and allowed him in, the tender muscles burning as they stretched to accommodate him. He eased in and out slowly, taking more of her with each thrust until he was all the way inside.

When he pressed those same three fingers back inside her weeping channel, she was stretched to the limit, full of him… he began to move his fingers and cock in tandem until she was lost in a sea of pleasure and pain that seemed to have no beginning and no end.

The pleasure built and built until it seemed to be growing to something she couldn't bear. "Taruk! I cannot! It's too much!"

"You can and you will! You will take everything I give you, then beg for more!" he said firmly as he began to move even more powerfully, forcing her to take the pleasure and the pain. Then the invisible band inside her snapped and catapulted her into orbit, her body clamping down on both his fingers and his cock and milking them hard.

He yelled hoarsely as he came, bathing her insides with his essence, leaving her marked in every orifice with his seed. Tyra found she did indeed feel owned… consumed by the beast. She was well pleased.

A MOMENT IN TIME

I writhed over your knee and gasped as your hand fell again and again, building the heat in my backside to unbelievable proportions.

"Oooh... owww... ohhhooo... please... oowww!" I cried, trying to rock my hips and bring my poor throbbing bottom out of the line of fire. It was to no avail; you held me fast, ensuring each and every swat found its target.

"Are you going to remember to behave yourself next time?" you asked as your hand fell in another barrage of swats.

"Yes, sir!" I wailed, tears filling my eyes as you began paying special attention to the area where my bottom met my thighs.

You delivered another ten to each sit spot, then lifted me to stand in front of you; I stood shifting from foot to foot, wanting nothing more than to rub my stinging bottom.

A firm finger beneath my chin forced my gaze to yours. "Are you sorry you were such a naughty girl?"

I sniffled, "Yes, sir."

You turned me away with another sharp swat. "Go stand in the corner and think about it; when you come out, you can show me how sorry you are for being such a bad girl."

I moved slowly to the corner, a little embarrassed to be standing there stark naked with a bright red bottom on display. I felt like a very well chastised little girl as I stood there glaring at the offending corner. Who came up with this punishment?

I hated the corner, it sucked. It truly had to be the most boring place on earth. I knew I was supposed to reflect on my behavior, but in reality I spent the whole time thinking about how much I hated the corner.

"Ready to show me how sorry you are, little girl?" you asked and I turned from the corner with an eager nod, smiling to see you lying back on our bed completely naked.

I climbed up on the bed and immediately took your hard cock into my mouth, paying special attention to the head, swirling my tongue around beneath it as I sucked.

"Show me your ass," you commanded and I obligingly shifted my position on the bed to straddle your chest facing away from you without relinquishing my prize.

You palmed my sore bottom, making me groan around your cock, then sank two fingers deep into my heat. I immediately rocked my hips back for more and was rewarded with two sharp swats on my already sore backside.

I took more and more of you into my mouth as my head bobbed on you; you tasted so good. Your fingers began to pump into me harder and harder as I sucked. Soon you were thrusting your hips up to meet my mouth, forcing your cock all the way to the back of my throat, making my eyes tear up as I gagged around you.

Your thumb began to play across my clit as your fingers pounded into me and then another finger slid smoothly into my ass. I felt my body begin to tighten as you overwhelmed my senses… filling my mouth, needy inner core, and my ass.

Harder and harder you took me everywhere, giving me no quarter… no escape… I moaned and hummed around your cock as you thrust aggressively into my mouth while your fingers pounded in and out of my body.

"Come now! Give it to me, it's mine," you ordered me,

and I came with a shudder and a soft scream around your cock just as you shot ribbon after ribbon of cum down my throat. I swallowed everything you gave me and continued to suck and lick, your cock moving slowly now as it rocked in and out.

I smiled around you as I realized you were hard and ready to go again. "Please... I'm sorry I was a bad girl...I want to come on your cock."

You pulled your fingers free of my still grasping body and started spanking me again. "Greedy girl."

I yelped but arched my bottom for you; now the slaps raining down were welcome and fueling my growing need to have you inside me.

I sucked you deep again, needing to have you inside me any way I could, then suddenly you pulled me off your cock and turned me to face you, impaling me to the hilt on your stiff cock.

"Ohhh," I cried out as you bumped my sensitive cervix, but you held me there and began to rotate your hips. The pleasure was so intense I couldn't do anything but feel, as you continued to move and grind high up inside me. Your thumb came down on my clit, rubbing it in a circular motion as you hit that magic spot inside again and again, the rough hair on your legs abrading my hot tender bottom... all of it coalescing together and overwhelming me completely.

I shattered above you, shuddering as my body exploded around you, and then my world tilted as you flipped me to my back.

You hooked my legs over your arms and began pounding in and out of me like a jackhammer; the different angle giving you different spots to hit inside of me and storming my defenses, shooting me straight from one orgasm to another, blending the pleasure together until there seemed to be no beginning and no end and I was lost in a sea of sensation.

Tears leaked from my eyes as I screamed your name, the heat of your seed splashing my inner walls as my body clamped down on your cock like it would never let go, milking you dry.

You groaned against my neck, holding me close as we both came back to earth, too spent to move, happy to lie together in the aftermath away from the rest of the world for a moment in time.

JUST MY IMAGINATION

Just my imagination... full of you and wishing you were here... I sigh as I sit in the tub, hot water gently gliding against my skin, skimming over my nipples. As they tighten in response, I imagine your lips sucking the moisture from the tightening buds...licking and sipping the water from my skin.

I lay back, my hands coming up to cup my breasts and pluck at my nipples until they are hard little points of need. In my mind I'm leaning against your chest and it's your hands rather than my own.

Your hand gliding down my stomach slowly and slipping between my legs, I moan and move my legs apart for you as your fingers glide smoothly between my lips, slightly grazing my clit.

Your thumb gently rubs against my clit in a circular motion as you send two fingers sinking deep into my aching heat. My back arches as you begin to use your fingers hard, giving my body no quarter... no escape from the demand in your touch.

You will have everything... I can deny you nothing. I feel your breath warm against my neck as you dip your head and lightly bite my earlobe, whispering, "When we get out of the tub, I'm going to bend you over the sink and spank your sweet ass till it glows and then I'm going to take everything that's mine over and over until you feel me every time you move tomorrow to remind you who you belong to."

I whimper as your fingers work my sheath hard, thrusting deep inside and hitting some magical spot while your thumb continues to worry my clit. Your fingers feel so good inside me... my body clamps down greedily as I begin to tremble, coming apart against you. You give me no respite, continuing to work my sheath.

"Give it to me... give me everything that's mine!" you command as your teeth close over my shoulder... the sweet pain shooting me over the edge completely... I cry out your name, an orgasm overwhelming me... my body shaking and quivering as my inner muscles milk your fingers.

"Good girl."

Your raspy voice sends another shiver of delight through me as you pull your fingers free from me and stroke them up my side soothingly.

My body is limp... replete... I smile as the water washes over my sensitive skin in a moist caress.

Slowly I come back to myself... alone... it was just my imagination running away with me...

YOUR GOOD GIRL

I stood in the corner, legs shoulder width apart, bent at the waist with my back arched to present my well spanked bottom and leave me open to whatever attentions you chose to give, my hands braced on either side of the corner my forehead rested against.

I shivered, naked and completely exposed… my bottom on fire with the heat centering in my clit and empty sheath, both throbbing and needy, a side effect of punishment.

Something deep inside me responded to your thorough mastery; it awakened the sexual beast at my core needing to be conquered and claimed.

I felt your warmth as you returned to me, one long finger sliding down my spine, leaving shivers in its wake. I gasped as your finger moved between my ass cheeks, skimming lightly over my tight rosebud then sliding into my wet heat.

I groaned as two fingers drove deep inside, my inner walls clamping down as if I could keep you where I needed you. Your fingers worked in and out of me as your thumb played across my clit. I could only give a breathless moan as I neared orgasm. It felt so good… then just as my body started to tighten down, you pulled free and delivered six sharp swats to each sit spot, leaving me gasping in a combination of need and pain.

"Please!" I wailed.

"Do naughty girls get to come?" you asked as if curious.

My shoulders slumped a little and I couldn't help the pout on my lips as I responded, "No, sir."

"Who gets to come?" you asked.

"Good girls," I answered without hesitation.

"Have you been a good girl?"

I sighed, "No, sir."

My reward for such honesty was a sharp swat to my bare mound; the sting sent me up on my toes and I bucked my hips reflexively as your fingers grazed my sensitive clit. Eight more swats landed and just when I thought I would go over the edge from your intimate discipline, once again you stopped, as I cried out in frustration.

You grabbed my hair, pulled my face up out of the corner for a minute, and leaned down to whisper in my ear, "You don't come until I give you permission, young lady. Am I understood?"

"Yes, sir." My words were almost a breathy sob. I was caught in a haze between pleasure and pain... my need to be taken, possessed almost overwhelming in its intensity.

Several more well placed swats on my already sore bottom brought tears to my eyes; my bottom felt so hot and stingy I was sure it was the color of a ripe tomato. I knew I'd feel your discipline every time I sat, well into the next day.

When your hands grasped my sore bottom cheeks and spread me open, it was all I could do to remain in position, the feel of your tongue driving into my pulsing channel making me want to grind against your face... I shook with the effort of staying where you placed me.

Again and again you brought me to the edge of orgasm only to deny me... until my tears were no longer from the pain of punishment but from a much deeper ache of need denied.

"Please... please... I'll be a good girl!" I shouted

hoarsely as once again you backed away just before I could come.

You lifted me to stand and turned me to face you, one hand cupping my chin and forcing my eyes to you. "Who does your body belong to?"

"You," I said breathlessly, sinking into the heat in your eyes.

"Who does your pleasure belong to?"

"You... only you," was my soft answer; my body was melting as the peace of my submission and your dominance wrapped around me... and I accepted once more your will as my own... no longer fighting my need to submit.

Your thumb wiped a lone tear from my cheek as you smiled down at me before kissing me tenderly. I sighed softly into your mouth as you gathered me close, then lifted me and laid me back on the bed. The sheets chafed my hot bottom, but I didn't care because you were fitting the head of your cock to my aching center and driving deep.

You continued to stare into my eyes as I welcomed you inside.

"Come now."

I exploded around you with a small scream. You stilled inside me for a moment before you started pounding into me hard and fast, every inward thrust catching my swollen clit and driving me closer and closer to another orgasm.

Words left me; I could only hang on to your shoulders as you took me with you into the maelstrom of pleasure, mewling little whimpers of pleasure my only sound. The release I was building toward became almost too much, but you would not be denied.

"Now!" you shouted and I could do nothing but obey as I shattered into a million pieces, your name a breathless sigh on my lips as I soared into orbit.

I returned to you, safe in your arms... ready to be your good girl again.

CLAIMED

She ran, her heart pounding in her throat as she heard his footsteps behind her. Though she knew she could never escape him, she had to make this attempt for freedom. Liana didn't want to be mated; she wanted to choose her own destiny.

Her father had told her many times that the day she met her mate, her future would be irrevocably bound to his, and she would have no choice regarding it. So she'd studiously avoided gatherings where she'd come into contact with males she'd never met.

Then he'd arrived in their village. Dare Merrick; she heard the people in the village whispering his name in awe as they talked of his prowess as a hunter. He was tall, dark, and devastatingly handsome... the brooding look on his face only added to his attractiveness. This was not a man to be trifled with; he would claim what he felt was his with no mercy. So when everything in her responded to just a glimpse of him and she'd known she was his, it struck fear into her core. When he turned toward her, lifting his head as if to catch a scent on the wind, she'd ducked down behind a shed.

Liana had avoided him at every turn, but today her time

had run out; he'd tracked her to her father's home. She'd gone out the back door as he'd come in the front; she'd scented him on the other side of the door.

She'd run despite his and her father's calls to stop, she had to try… he would consume her… change her… and while part of her melted at the thought, another part of her was terrified. These feelings were too much… too strong… too everything.

Liana knew she'd run faster as a wolf, so she began stripping her clothes as she ran; she'd just shed her jeans when he caught up to her, moving to block her path.

"You will stop, little mate, before I grow more unhappy with you," Dare said firmly. The shadow of a beard lining his jaw made him appear even more menacing.

Liana flushed guiltily. "Why would you be unhappy with me?"

He snorted. "You know exactly why, young lady. I scented you when I came into town over a week ago. You've been hiding from me ever since. I didn't finally find you until today and you made matters worse by running from me."

"I… ummm…I wasn't exactly…" she began.

"Enough! You will not lie to me! You scented me in the same moment I did you; I smelt more than the scent of my mate in the air that day, little girl," Dare growled as he backed her toward a tree.

Liana's heartbeat sped up even faster and her breath started coming in pants as she felt a flood of moisture spring forth between her thighs. "What do you mean?"

He laughed as he bent over her where she now stood with her back against the tree and ran his lips up the side of her neck as she arched it for him with a low groan. "I scented your arousal on the wind… the spicy scent of my mate in need; just as I smell it now."

He kissed her deeply and her soft body yielded sweetly against him after one mewling cry of protest, "No…"

"Yes, little mate. Your body cries out to me, it sings to

my senses of how great your need is; it is a call that cannot go unanswered." This time when he kissed her, she responded with complete abandon, letting go of her fears and cares, giving him everything he demanded.

Liana tried to follow him when he pulled away. "What?" she asked with a little frown when he shook his head at her with a chuckle.

"First we must deal with the fact that you avoided me, ran from me, and then tried to deny it. These crimes will be dealt with before I take what is rightfully mine," Dare told her firmly.

She glared up at him. "You will do no such thing!"

He shook his head and then bent at the waist to catch her midsection on his shoulder before he straightened and started back the way they'd come.

The warm palm of his hand rested on her panty-clad bottom, patting warningly when she would have protested further.

The journey back to the village was made in silence and he carried her through the center of town with all of her friends and neighbors witnessing her slung over his shoulder like a sack of potatoes. No one would intervene; technically she'd broken pack law by running from her mate.

Dare ducked inside the building he'd made his temporary home, dumping her on the bed. "Strip."

"I... can't we talk about this?" she asked hesitantly.

"The time for talking about your fears was a week and a half ago; instead you chose to behave like a child and now you will receive a child's consequences. But I will spank you as a woman... it's a mate's punishment you will receive," he told her in an implacable tone.

Tears gathered in her eyes as she stripped off her top, then her bra and panties, leaving her completely bare to his gaze.

Dare sat down on the bed. "Place yourself across my lap."

Taking a deep breath, Liana lay over his lap, groaning in

embarrassment as he parted her legs so that one rested on either side of his thigh, leaving her completely open to him. Her upper torso was bent beneath his arm, holding her firmly in place as his hand began to pepper her backside.

He left not one inch of skin untouched, his hand falling again and again relentlessly until she was wailing beneath his arm.

Her bottom felt like it was swollen to three times its normal size by the time he was satisfied and then two fingers drove deep into her wet and aching sheath.

Liana's sob of pain changed to one of pleasure as his fingers began to pump in and out of her in a firm rhythm. The heat and pain in her bottom seemed to entwine with the pleasure he was providing until they were one, each stroke of his hand bringing her higher and higher until she was sure she would explode with pleasure. He stopped just before she could come, and then he put her on the floor on her hands and knees.

She whimpered a plea as she pressed her chest to the floor, spreading her legs wide for him. It was an invitation it seemed he could not resist as he fitted the head of his cock to her slick opening and slammed home in one hard thrust.

Liana came almost immediately as he filled her, but Dare continued to move, slamming all the way inside and then withdrawing almost completely before slamming inside again.

He rode her hard, pistoning in and out of her like a jackhammer over and over, until she lost track of the number of orgasms she'd had. Her voice now gave only raspy cries, raw from screaming her pleasure; the pleasure that it seemed would kill her before it came to an end.

By the time Dare bit into her shoulder as he came hard inside her, splashing her inner walls with his hot seed, sending her into one more shattering climax, Liana was irrevocably his… claimed so completely she was certain she'd feel him every time she breathed from this day forward.

Surprisingly, she found she would have it no other way.

TAKE ME HARD

I hung up the phone in the lobby with a smile, knowing I'd made you as hungry for me as I was for you. The cool breeze drifting up my skirt and hitting my bare, wet mound only magnified the ache in my clit; I could feel my arousal dripping down my inner thighs.

It was a two-edged sword, this teasing game I played; lighting your fire stoked my furnace as well. I needed you inside me so badly now, it was all I could do to stay upright in the elevator.

As I watched the numbers in the elevator get closer and closer to your floor, my heartbeat grew faster, pounding in my ears and between my thighs. I could almost hear the beat as it thrummed, "take me… take me…"

Finally, I was at your door, sliding the card key into the slot when the door swung open forcefully and there you were, grabbing me and pulling me inside. I barely had time to register your open shirt and unfastened pants before I found myself thrust back against a wall.

"I…" was all you allowed before your mouth swooped down to cover mine, devouring me as if you'd swallow me whole. Your tongue swept inside, reclaiming what was yours, determinedly conquering my own until I just followed where you led, as you swallowed the soft mewling little cries I couldn't contain.

You jerked the material of my skirt up over my hips, then lifted me at the waist and my legs instinctively wrapped around your hips as you drove inside me to the hilt.

"Ooooh," I cried as you began to pound relentlessly in and out of my heat, my back slammed into the wall every time you drove inside, but I didn't care. My head fell back on my shoulders.

Then your arms came up under mine and your hands cupped my head. "No, you will look at me. Who owns you?" you rasped hoarsely.

My eyes were trapped in your piercing gaze as you sank into me. "You do."

You continued to stare down into my eyes as you drove my body up higher and higher until I shattered around you with a quiet scream, but still you pounded into me, sending me from one peak straight into another, the connection between us palpable; I was unable to look away.

It was as if you possessed me body and soul; I knew in that moment as you commanded my body to come again and again there against the wall that I'd been forever altered.

You owned me completely and utterly; I'd never belong to myself again.

"Come for me, give me everything that is mine," you commanded and I came apart so completely in your arms, I could do nothing but scream your name as the orgasm you wrenched from me was almost more intense than I could bear.

Then you gently kissed the tears of pleasure from my cheeks and lowered me to stand on still quivering legs. "Good girl. Now we'll discuss your punishment for calling me from the lobby to tell me you weren't wearing panties."

I leaned weakly against you but still managed to look up at you with an unrepentant smile. "Yes, sir."

A LESSON IN SELF-DISCIPLINE

When you called me, I was so excited. I hate when you're out of town on business. Then you asked how my writing was going and my stomach dropped to my feet.

Since I'd left my job to write full time, you'd had very serious expectations about my productivity.

"If you're going to write full time, young lady, it will be your job and you should take it just as seriously," you said sternly.

"Of course I will!" I'd promised so brightly, and I did well when you were home and keeping an eye on me, but when you were away...

"Umm... things haven't gone so well this week. I... I only completed one chapter." I bit my lip as I waited for your reaction.

"One chapter the entire time I've been away? What about the revisions your editor has been waiting for? Did you at least finish those?" The displeasure in your tone made me want to cry.

"Not exactly..." I hedged.

"Did you exactly send her anything?"

"No, sir," I said softly.

"Did you finish any revisions?" you asked.

I sighed and closed my eyes before answering, "No, sir."

"I believe a very firm lesson in self-discipline is called for as soon as I get home." A shudder went through me at the implacability in your tone.

I crave your punishment as much as I dread it. Sometimes I wonder if I misbehave on purpose, just to get a little of that stern attention that feeds the dark need deep inside me.

"I'm sorry," I told you earnestly though I knew you'd grant me no amnesty.

"We shall see. I'll be home to pick you up at six; be ready to go. Wear the green dress I just bought you."

"What? We're going out? But I thought…"

"Yes. We're going out, and darling?"

"Yes, sir?"

"No panties." The call disconnected and I was left reeling. I was being taken out to dinner. You weren't going to punish me? I felt bereft… were you so displeased with me, I was no longer worth your correction?

So many thoughts ran through my mind as I got ready for our evening out. Surely you hadn't grown tired of me and hadn't given up on me. I needed you like I needed the air; without you, I didn't think I could survive.

I knew that was dramatic. I would survive, but my life would go back to like it was before I met you. Empty loneliness would stretch out before me as I went through the motions of living. In many ways I felt like I'd been born when I met you, because that was truly when I came to life.

I studied my reflection in the mirror; the green high-waisted dress lifted and hugged my breasts before flowing around my legs in a loose swirl of material. Cool air teased up my thighs and between my legs as I moved, completely naked beneath the dress as you'd instructed me.

My makeup was carefully applied, giving my wide brown eyes a luminous look, accenting the color riding high on my cheeks and the full pout of my lips. I twisted up my blond hair in an elegant French twist that left my neck and shoulders bare.

Then you were behind me in the mirror and I turned to greet you, throwing myself into your embrace.

"I've missed you," I said, pressing myself as close to you as possible, like you could absorb me into your being.

You gave me a tight squeeze and kissed the top of my head before setting me away from you. "I've missed you too, baby, but you've been very naughty, haven't you?"

Immediately wet heat sprang to life between my thighs; you hadn't given up on me. "Yes, sir."

"We need to work on your self-discipline, don't we, little girl?" you asked with a raised brow.

I shuddered as you ran one hand lightly down my arm. "Yes, sir."

You nodded as if satisfied with my response. "Good girl. Let's go to dinner."

Confusion filled me as you took my arm and led me outside to the car. I didn't understand what was happening, but heat was curling deep within my core. Something momentous was about to occur; I just had no idea what.

During the ride to the restaurant, you talked about a little bit of everything, but really nothing of importance. I found it difficult to follow the thread of the conversation because I was so worried about the consequences of my actions. Obviously you had more than a quick spanking in mind.

When the waiter seated us at a table at the darkened end of the terrace, secluded from the other diners, my pulse quickened.

Our chairs were against the back wall, close together rather than on opposite sides of the table. It was a very intimate seating.

The waiter placed menus on the table then left us; you smiled at me and then stood. "Stand up, please."

I frowned and rose to stand next to you. As I watched, you unfolded a napkin and laid it over the chair seat. Then, pulling me close to you, you began to gather the back of my skirt up in your hands until I felt air against my naked bottom.

"What are you doing?" I asked in alarm.

"No one can see you," you assured me softly. "Sit down."

I sat my naked bottom on the napkin and you artfully draped my dress around my seated body, covering me completely.

You smiled rather mysteriously as you pulled a wrapped object from your pocket. I couldn't tell what it was, but when I asked, you only told me to wait and see, then picked up your menu.

I squirmed in nervous anticipation, the wet heat between my thighs increasing my distraction.

The waiter returned and we ordered our food; I had never been able to focus on the menus so you finally sighed and ordered for me.

"Focus is a large part of self-discipline," was all you said in admonishment and I blushed.

While we were eating our salads, you stopped eating and unwrapped the package you'd laid on the table.

I gasped; it was a long thick finger of peeled ginger in a crooked L shape, the short leg of the L coming off the longest leg at its broadest end at a funny angle. Heat filled my face as my eyes darted nervously around the restaurant.

"Eyes on me, no one can see you," you told me firmly.

My eyes sprang to yours as I waited. "Are you wet for me?"

I blushed fiercely but nodded.

"Use your words, please," you said.

"Yes, sir, I'm wet for you." I squeaked the words out through suddenly dry lips.

"Open your legs for me," you instructed as you placed a hand on my thigh.

"You can't do this here! We're in public," I exclaimed, alarmed but more aroused than I'd ever been in my life.

"I can be discreet. If you're wet, and I know you are, it means you're enjoying this."

I groaned and moved my legs apart as I felt your hand slide under my skirts, the ginger gone from the table. Biting my lip, I spread my legs even further apart when I felt the blunt tip of the ginger slide inside my quivering sheath.

"You've never used ginger there before," I whimpered, nervous about the heat I knew I would be feeling soon.

"There's a first time for everything," you said with a low chuckle that brought goosebumps to the surface of my skin.

Then you began to move the thick root in and out of me slowly, only giving me an inch or so with each slow thrust. I whimpered and began to buck up to meet you, hungry for a deeper penetration.

"Ahh-ahhh," you scolded me quietly. "This is an exercise in self-discipline, young lady. You will remain still and take what I give you. No more… no less."

My breath rushed out in a shuddering sigh as I forced my needy body to stay still. "Yes, sir."

"Good girl," you said, a faint smile on your lips as you began to work it deeper and deeper inside me.

My slick fluids began to mix with the ginger's own juices, making it easy for you to thrust it almost all the way inside as you began to take me with a hard rhythm. I bit my lip hard to keep from crying out as I contracted around the root and began to feel its fiery essence sinking into my tender tissues.

"It burns," I softly whined in complaint.

"Breathe through it, the discomfort will pass," you said as you sank it the rest of the way inside me, pressing the short leg between my swollen lips, the knobby end coming to rest against my throbbing clit.

At my soft moan, you pressed it against me again and again, almost gently but awakening the burn between my tender lips and clit.

Then just as I thought I was about to come, despite the slight discomfort of the heat now filling me and dripping down to my anus as I helplessly grew wetter and wetter, you removed your hand completely and went back to your salad.

I wanted to hump myself on the chair, pressing the root deeper inside me and causing friction against my clit, but I knew better.

"No squirming, young lady. Remember, self-discipline. Now eat your salad."

Holding as still as possible I began to nibble at my salad, but wasn't able to eat much with all my focus centered between my legs. I was unable to keep from occasionally clenching against the ginger and sending a jolt of painful pleasure through my loins but I did try, knowing if I clenched too many times I'd come and then be in more trouble than I already was.

Dinner seemed to take forever; by the time you'd paid the check I was in such a heightened state of arousal I wanted to weep with my need.

You helped me to my feet and instructed me not to lose the ginger. Walking slowly and carefully to the car, I managed to keep it in place inside me, clenching my muscles tightly around the root, increasing the intensity of the burn in the process.

You seated me in the car and leaned in to whisper in my ear, "If you can come before I get to my seat, you are free to do so."

Needing no further invitation, I clenched my muscles tightly around the ginger and bounced hard on my seat, shoving the ginger deeper inside hard and making it rub my clit. I was so primed, it only took two bounces before I was coming with a little scream, my back bowing as I convulsed tightly around the root, releasing more of its fiery oils.

It took the edge off my need, but wasn't nearly enough; I'd started to bounce in my seat ready to come again when you sat down next to me. "No. One was enough; you don't get to come again until my cock is planted in your ass."

Your dark words were almost enough to send me over the edge, but I bit my lip sharply, allowing the little pain to help me gain control of myself again.

"When we get home, you will go immediately to the

living room, take your dress off, and bend over the arm of the couch. I will give you ten licks from the tawse after you ask me to punish you hard with it. Then I will take your ass while I use the ginger to work your tender quim."

I closed my eyes and moaned at the image your words invoked.

"What do you think of this lesson in self-discipline, love?"

"I think it's very effective sir," I said earnestly, already having decided I'd rather have a spanking every day than this relentless teasing. Making me wait and be still while the ginger root worked its magic on me was agony. I was a mass of aching need.

Finally, we arrived home and I moved quickly… glad to rid myself of my dress and the feel of the material sliding against my heavy breasts… stroking against my naked ass in a whispery caress.

I bent almost eagerly over the arm of the couch, my legs spread apart as I knew you'd expect, the couch pressing enticingly against the ginger, which caused it to press against me.

Every stroke of the tawse would sweetly combine the pain of my punishment with pleasure as it forced me harder against the wicked root.

Then you were there, tawse in hand; you stood behind me waiting.

I knew what you wanted. "Please punish me hard with the tawse, sir."

You didn't make me wait any longer, the tawse falling in a line of fire on my vulnerable bottom. I yelped as my hips bucked reflexively against the arm of the couch, shooting a flare of pleasure through my clit and pulsing sheath even as I gasped at the pain.

Stroke after stroke fell hard against my bottom, each one bringing me closer and closer to orgasm even as tears began to fall from my eyes. My bottom burned from the middle of my ass to just below the swell of my cheeks by the time all ten strokes had been laid down.

Then I heard your zipper and you spread my tender bottom cheeks wide as the thick head of your cock pressed against my shy little anus.

You were able to coat yourself generously in the juices of my desire coating my thighs and sank easily into my ass as I pressed greedily back against you. Needing you... needing your mastery at this most base level.

I felt myself opening to you like a flower to the sun as I surrendered everything to you. When you pressed all the way inside, I came screaming around you as the fire in my clit exploded against the intense pressure of the root, then you began to ride me hard.

Reaching around me, you caught the short piece of the root and began working it in and out of me in tandem with your hard thrusts, grazing my clit with every inward stroke. Soon I was convulsing around you and milking your shaft in an almost endless orgasm.

It seemed I came ceaselessly until finally you released inside me with one last lunge and a loud groan.

I shuddered and shivered beneath you, caught up in the aftermath of the intensity of your lesson. Ever so gently you pulled out of me and removed the ginger before lifting my limp sated body in your arms.

"Thank you, sir," I whispered softly into your neck as I wrapped my arms around you, thankful to have you home again.

THE ACHE

I ache… my body throbs with a need only you can assuage… when I move my legs restlessly, the pressure it puts on my sensitive clit causes me to whimper out loud.

You chuckle as if amused by my need, but as you approach our bed where I'm waiting, the heat in your eyes tells another story. You need me as badly as I ache for you.

You tease us both with your control; I shiver as your eyes slide over my naked flesh and I thrill at the possessiveness in your gaze.

"Please?" I whisper softly. Begging with my eyes for you to give me relief, knowing you will do so in your own time. I know you enjoy making me wait… drawing out and magnifying my need until I'm insensate… almost becoming a wild thing in your arms.

When I think I will go mad before you give me what has become more necessary than air, you send me to the stars and beyond. The game changes completely as you demand everything I am… sending my body into orgasm again and again, until the pleasure is almost painful in its ruthless intensity.

My mind is not allowed to interfere with thoughts of other things; my body knows its master… the man it belongs to. Sometimes it takes but a glance from you to start a pulse of need beating between my thighs, awakening that thing inside me that had lain dormant for so long before we met.

I never completely understood need and desire before that moment... having no idea what it meant to ache to be filled with another person so badly, the emptiness of your core echoes through you with a need strong enough to reduce you to tears.

Now I do... when you are inside me I feel complete... I love everything about the way your cock stretches me open and molds my body to yours... the way you cover me... your larger, stronger body wrapping me as you take me... leaving me headily aware of the ease with which you could crush me... yet you are my anchor... my strength... my safety.

I love the differences between us... your hardness where I am soft... the friction of your hair-roughened skin sliding against the smoothness of my own... your scent seems to cocoon me in its embrace... the contrast between my stern task master, my demanding lover, and the tender way you hold me close in the aftermath of passion, like you would protect me from all harm.

My body being flipped forcibly over brings me back to awareness. I jerk as a sharp swat lands on my now upturned bottom.

"Do I have your attention again?" Your deep husky voice rolls over me in an invisible caress.

"Yes, sir," I say softly, completely back with you... ready for whatever you have in store. I smile to myself.

You own my heart and soul... I am completely yours, but you are also mine.

SAFE IN YOU

I stood at the edge of the cemetery and watched as people slowly made their way back to the waiting cars. Tears unchecked ran down my cheeks as I considered all the dreams that would never be realized.

Such a tragedy to lose life at such a young age, so unfair... to die before there was even a chance to really live. Seventeen and gone... Savannah had been one of the most alive people I'd ever met.

Bright and beautiful... always smiling even though her small body was often racked with pain. It saddened me to know I would never see the absolute joy that filled her smile again, but it was the thought of her mother's pain that almost brought me to my knees.

During the service she'd held herself tall, not crumpling until the very end when the time had come to lower the coffin. That last moment of goodbye had left her undone and she'd collapsed into her husband's arms as they mourned their loss.

To share such moments of unspeakable grief with others formed a bond that left people connected. It's not something you speak of or an intimacy you discuss because those moments leave you naked, exposed to the bone.

I could not imagine what Savannah's parents were going through, but I hoped they were able to find some solace in the fact that she was no longer in pain. The thought of that bright ray of sunshine dancing around heaven on sturdy pain-free legs made me smile through my tears.

I sighed and wiped the tears from my face as I walked slowly to my own car. The drive home was made in a daze; I didn't even remember the journey when I pulled into our driveway.

It was a surprise to walk in the door and see you standing there, my rock... my haven when life's storms rocked me to my core. "I thought you'd still be at work."

"Not when you need me," you said quietly as you opened your arms wide.

I flew to you, throwing myself into your arms, the tears starting again before you could even wrap them completely around me. "She was so young."

"I know," you said softly as you held me and rocked me to and fro. No further words were spoken as you simply held me and let me cry it out. Finally, my tears spent, I looked up at you with a wobbly smile.

"I need you to possess me so completely I don't know where you end and I begin," I told you huskily, knowing you could chase away the shadows and remind me of the joy that can be shared between two people who love each other as we do.

You firmly caught the back of my head between your hands and devoured me with your eyes before leaning in to take my mouth, making it yours. Owning me completely in this moment in time, taking what was yours.

Firm hands set me away; I swayed, slightly disoriented, drugged on your kiss alone. "Strip," you said succinctly and I rushed to comply.

When I stood naked before you, a hand came out to stroke down the left side of my body in a fleeting caress, leaving me shivering with need.

"Bend over the arm of the couch." Your stern words

rolled over me, feeding the darker need inside me even as I looked at you questioningly.

"Why?" I asked softly.

"Because you need it," was your simple answer.

Before I knew it I was in place and your hand was falling hard and fast on my upturned bottom. As the heat and sting grew, I realized you were right; I did need this almost as much as I needed you.

Again and again your hand fell until tears were once again falling unchecked down my cheeks. This thing we do is interesting; though my bottom was now on fire, I was also getting wetter and wetter as the ache between my thighs grew.

I whimpered softly and looked over my shoulder beseechingly at you. "Please…"

The sound of your pants being undone and hitting the floor filled the silence in the room and then you were there filling me with your cock, giving me what I so desperately needed. Soon I was completely lost in you and your touch.

You possessed me utterly, without mercy, but in return you gave everything inside you. One firm hand slid around to cup my mound and spread me even wider as you pressed my clit against the glide of your cock.

Each time you pounded into me, my clit rode both your cock and fingers, stroking it from each side until I shattered completely in your arms, screaming your name. You came with me, nipping me lightly on the back of the neck as you filled me with your seed.

You gathered me carefully against you and lowered us both to the floor as we came back to ourselves. I snuggled into your warmth… safe… in my heart and my home… in you.

TAMRYN'S TAMING

She ran quickly, her bare feet carrying her as fast as possible as she made her way up the rocky incline. He would be looking for her; she had to put as much ground as possible between herself and the husband her family had given her over to just this very morn.

He confused and frightened her... everything about him was too much. He was too big... too imposing... his torso tattooed like a Pict though he wore the kilt of a Scotsman.

Her father had told her the man demanded something from the village to prove their loyalty to him as their new overlord. The something turned out to be her; he'd seen her around the village and felt she'd make a good bride.

As Tamryn had looked up into his dark eyes during the ceremony forever joining her life to his, she'd known she couldn't do it. His eyes consumed her and she knew if he took her, she would be forever altered. He would change her fundamentally... he would consume everything she was and nothing would ever be the same again.

So Tamryn had run; she'd been left to wait in a tent for her new husband and she'd crawled out the back and headed straight toward the forest and the cliffs hoping to find refuge from her fate.

She understood why her father had given her to him...
Barrik the Overlord. Theirs was a small village, a simple
people; they wouldn't survive an attack. None of their men
were warriors... just farmers, providing for their families as
much as possible with their barren lands.

As she scrambled up another steep incline, Tamryn
grasped the branch of a nearby tree to pull herself up and
then she heard him on the ground beneath her rocky perch.

His deep voice carried to her on the wind. "Come to me,
my little mouse... I grow weary of your games."

She shivered and clutched frantically at the branch as she
tried to climb faster, then she heard a snapping sound and
she was falling backwards.

Tamryn screamed as she fell, fearing this was her end,
but instead of hitting the jagged rocks below her, a hard
body broke her fall.

Barrik caught her high against him, let out a battle cry of
victory, and then laughed as he looked down into her pale
face. "You'll not escape me that easily, little mouse. I would
fight the devil himself to keep what is mine... and you,
Tamryn of Camerdoone, are definitely mine."

"No..." she said, finding her voice for the first time to
protest.

"You will not deny me, wife," Barrik said sternly. "At
least not for long. I keen you are frightened by this thing
that rests between us. You do not yet understand its power
and the power of the passion that rests inside you, little one,
but you will."

Tamryn struggled futilely against his hold. "Nay... there
is naught between us!"

Barrik laughed again. "Yes, and you keen it... that is why
you ran... it frightens you, but fear not, my little mouse; the
fire may well consume us both but I will not let it burn you."

She shuddered helplessly in his arms, her wide blue eyes
trapped in the darkness of his gaze. She tried shaking her
head at him again, but he merely laughed and carried her to
the spot where his horse was tethered at the edge of the

wood.

"Yes, little wife… yes… that is all I will hear from your sweet lips soon… that and please," he said with a feral grin.

He stood her by his horse and stripped her naked, then tied her hands to the pommel of his saddle. "You will wait here while I ready our resting place for the night."

Tamryn's eyes widened as she stood helpless and naked before him, completely bared to his gaze and from the look in his eyes it was a view he enjoyed. Then with another smirk he turned away to build a fire and spread a blanket he pulled from the back of his saddle.

He planned to rut with her on the ground like an animal! She pulled sharply at the ties on her wrists, dismayed at the wetness she felt springing forth between her legs. What was wrong with her? She could not want this man… could she?

"It is time, Tamryn; I will wait no longer to make you fully mine," he said as he came to her and lifted her bound hands free of the saddle.

He pulled her round to stand next to the fire, and studied her worried face before sliding down to peruse her full breasts, her narrow waist that flared into full womanly hips, the soft thatch of dark blond hair that hid her secrets… the glint of moisture shining in the firelight on her thigh.

He smiled again then jerked her against him as he loosened the kilt at his waist and pulled Tamryn to her knees as he sank down to the ground, the loose material of his kilt blowing to wrap around his legs and hers as if tying them together.

Barrik went to one knee and pulled her to him, his other leg pressed tightly against her hip as her bound hands were pressed to his chest and he caught her thick blond tresses in his fist to pull her head back.

She moaned and shivered in response to the fire that began to lick through her veins as his lips met the sensitive skin of her neck.

His mouth licked and nipped at every inch of skin open to him, working his way down her neck and along her collarbone before moving up and claiming her mouth in a kiss meant to conquer… to claim… to consume.

Of their own accord her traitorous lips opened to his marauding tongue, allowing him entry to claim her mouth as his own. He consumed her lips, then his tongue plunged deep once more, stroking along her own and tempting it into a dance as old as time as they twined together.

Soon her hands were no longer pushing him away but clinging to his chest, kneading every bit of skin she could reach as she sank into him, surrendering to the need he stirred inside her.

When his fingers slid down her bare stomach and came to rest in the nest of curls between her thighs, she moaned and moved her legs apart.

She was so slick his finger slid inside effortlessly, moving back and forth as the pad of his thumb teased her clit. Her bound hands began to clench helplessly on his shoulder as her hips rode his finger.

Barrik chuckled and added a second finger to increase the friction and stretch her open for him. "That's it, little mouse, ride my hand."

Tamryn's head fell back as she rode his fingers harder and harder, searching for something she didn't understand but was on the pinnacle of discovering.

Just as her body began to tighten slightly around his fingers, Barrik pulled them free of her, making her cry out in protest as he snatched away whatever it was she'd been reaching for. "Nooo!"

He laughed again. "You'll get there, love, but not until I allow it; first you must answer for running from your husband."

Then she found herself straddling his knee and bent forward under one strong arm. Her balance felt precarious and she clutched at the back of his thigh for support. She gasped when the first swat landed on her upturned bottom, stinging heat filling the area as a jolt of pleasure hit her clit where it pressed against his knee.

On and on he spanked her; the heated pain in her bottom grew with every well placed swat, but each swat also gave her a jolt of pleasure. Soon the pain and pleasure were so intertwined she almost couldn't tell them apart, though she knew she would feel the spanking every time she sat for the next few days.

Barrik spanked her hard and fast until tears fell from her eyes while she moaned in pleasure… it was confusing, but she wanted more.

Tamryn found herself lifted from his knee and laid on her back before the fire, the warm woolen blanket beneath her aggravating the tender flesh of her punished backside. In no time at all her hands were secured above her head to a stake in the ground she hadn't noticed.

Barrik stood over her and studied his captured prize. Her heart sprang to her throat at the look in his eyes. Tamryn's breath quickened as he bent over her bound form.

"My pretty, pretty bride," Barrik said as he ran a hand lightly down the side of her body, bringing a shiver in its wake. "So responsive, soon you'll be able to take my cock anyway I choose, but today I've got something traditional in mind."

She swallowed as she studied his cock; it was long and thick, the head red and angry-looking where it stood out from his body with a bit of moisture leaking out the tip. Just yesterday the sight would have sent her screaming away from the man, but today there was just the sweet need he'd awakened in her body and an answering pulse pounding between her legs.

Tamryn licked her lips with anticipation.

He came down over her slowly, teasingly… touching her everywhere at once… his caresses so light and fleeting. She found herself straining to move toward him but couldn't with his body holding her legs down and her hands stretched above her head.

"Please," she whimpered as frustrated tears filled her eyes.

A hand gently stroked down her cheek as he smiled into her eyes. "How can I resist such a pretty plea?"

She gasped when one large hand plumped her breast and then his lips fastened around her nipple. What was he doing? Then he began to suckle like a babe… but harder and suddenly she didn't care.

"Ooooh…" Tamryn couldn't believe how good his mouth felt at her breast; a direct line seemed to go from her nipple to the pulse pounding so demandingly at the apex of her thighs.

As he suckled, his hand moved back between her legs and those two fingers thrust back inside her firmly. The combination was all she needed to shoot over the edge she'd been balancing on… her mouth opened in an 'oh' of surprise as she cried out in pleasure beneath his knowing touch.

"Good girl," he said, moving to latch onto the other breast and give it the same treatment as his fingers continued to pump in and out of her. Soon she was lost in sensation as he worked her body up to a frenzied pitch again.

This time as she shot over the edge he moved down her body and caught her clit in his mouth, sucking it hard.

Tamryn screamed as she went straight from one orgasm into another and still he gave her no rest, continuing to worry the little knot of nerves and work his fingers in and out hard.

Her breath was coming in desperate pants, her body immobile beneath him. "I can't…" she wailed as her body seemed to move toward an impossible peak.

"You can and you will," he said sternly, feeling her body begin to tighten around his fingers before he removed them and moved quickly up her body to capture her mouth with his own as he drove his rigid cock deep inside.

She barely felt the pain of his entry as his body speared hers to the hilt; he'd caught her knees on his arms, spreading her wide as he drove inside, then stilled inside her. Tamryn felt pierced to the core of her very soul as she looked up into his eyes.

Something shifted inside her and she knew things had forever changed, she was completely his... he would never let her go.

Barrik looked down at her as he growled, "Mine!"

Then he began to move, taking her fiercely and winding the invisible bow inside her tighter and tighter with every stroke of his cock and caress of his hand until she came completely undone in his arms.

Tamryn's back arched as she screamed his name in a release that seemed to go on and on... completely destroying the child she now felt like she'd been and reforming her into a woman... Barrik's woman.

His body slammed into her one final time and his head buried in her neck as he emptied himself into her, giving her everything he was as surely as he'd taken her all.

They lay there for a long moment, heartbeat to heartbeat as their breathing returned to normal. Then Barrik pulled free from her body; he smiled as he stroked a gentle hand through her hair before releasing her hands.

Tamryn whimpered as the blood came back into her wrists; he gently rubbed them until the feeling passed then pulled her exhausted body back into his before covering them both with his kilt.

She sighed, liking the way her body felt pressed against him, one of her legs resting between his while the other wrapped around his hip.

A less than gentle slap landed on her still sore bottom, bringing her eyes up to his with a gasp.

"You will never run from me again, wife."

Tamryn blinked. "No, sir."

"I promise if you do, or if you give me cause to punish you again, you will find no pleasure in it a second time," he warned her seriously.

A slight smile came to her lips as she looked up at him. "Yes, husband," she said softly as she laid her head down on his chest and snuggled in tight. She was no longer afraid of her barbarian husband and what the future held.

She was exactly where she was meant to be, safe in his arms.

THE MUSIC IN ME

I swayed to the music in a quiet corner just outside the room, hoping no one noticed me. It was an energetic group; the young people spun around the room laughing as they danced. I tried to remember a time when I'd been so carefree, but there really wasn't one.

The music spoke to me though, on some level I didn't completely understand. The wild beat thrumming through my system found an echo within me. I wanted to dance... to sing... to spin around the room like an uncontrolled top, without a care in the world.

Sighing, I made myself stop moving to the beat. I wanted to do these things but I never would... there wasn't any sense in imagining it.

"Working late, Anna?" A deep voice spoke from just behind me, causing me to jump.

I spun around my hand at my throat and gasped when I saw my boss, Eric, watching me, his eyes veiled by the shadows.

"I... what?" I asked, embarrassed by the thought he'd seen me living vicariously through the youthful party in the ballroom.

"Working late again?" he asked as he stepped forward

into the light, his chocolate brown gaze locking onto my face.

"No… I was about to head home. I just…"

"Wanted to dance?" Eric said with a smile.

"No. I don't dance," I said with a frown.

He moved almost before I saw him and pulled me into his arms. "Sure you do, Anna. I've seen the way you respond to the music. It's not good to deny yourself; in fact, I've decided I won't do it any longer."

"I really don't think this is a good idea," I said nervously as he spun me around the hallway, and I made a halfhearted attempt to pull away, which he firmly checked.

"You will dance with me, Anna," he said sternly, capturing my gaze once more.

The beat of the music leapt into my veins, my heart suddenly pounding along with it as if keeping time. It was intoxicating… being swung around the room in the arms of one of the most handsome men I knew.

I let the music take me and gave myself over to my masterful partner. When the music slowed he pulled me in close, halting for a moment. As I rested against him, time seemed to stand still.

A gentle hand lifted my chin so I was staring once more into the depths of his dark eyes. I felt trapped, completely captivated by what I saw there… stark need… a need that seemed to mirror my own.

Eric's hand stroked lightly down my cheek as he leaned in and placed a soft kiss against my lips. Then he smiled and let me go; taking my hand, he led me down the hall. Away from the party… away from prying eyes… he pulled me after him into the big study where he did most of his business.

My much smaller office was a few doors down, where I typed his notes and kept up with his busy schedule.

Eric let go of my hand as he closed the door after us; silence filled the room. My heart was now beating so fast I thought it might burst. Surely he could hear it; it seemed so loud in the quiet.

"You've been very naughty, Anna," he told me softly.

A flush of heat filled me at his words, a pool of moisture springing forth between my thighs. It was as if he'd read my most secret thoughts... dark needs and cravings I never dared to voice. It frightened me a little and I started to back away.

"No." The word was quietly spoken, but the command was still implicit and I froze in place.

"I..." I couldn't think of anything to say, really... it had just been an attempt to fill the gap and close the silence between us.

"There's no need to speak, Anna. As I said, you've been very naughty and I plan to remedy that immediately," Eric said calmly.

I blinked up at him, hardly daring to hope this was really happening. Shaking my head as if to clear it, I almost laughed at myself; I was being silly. He was probably about to chew me out for some major clerical errors on his correspondence, but I had to ask. "How?"

"I'm going to spank you, of course, Anna. It's long overdue. I'm going to turn you over my knee and spank your bare bottom for denying yourself so many things over the years and then I'm going to bend you over that desk and make you mine." The words were spoken with such surety I almost came spontaneously at the imagery they invoked. "You know you need a spanking, don't you?"

My mouth was suddenly dry, in stark contrast to the veritable lake welling up between my thighs. It might have been crazy, but I was going to do everything he asked of me. Perhaps in the light of day it would prove to be a mistake and I'd lose my job, but I'd have a memory to think about when I was alone again in my twin bed.

"Answer me, Anna," Eric said sharply.

"Yes, sir," I said, soft as a whisper.

"Yes, sir, what?" he prompted.

"Yes, sir, I need a spanking," I said boldly, meeting his

gaze straight on.

He smiled warmly at me, chasing away all my fears. "Strip."

As if in a dream I did as he asked, unfastening my dress and slipping it from my body, then removing my bra and panties. I stood there shivering and naked except for my heels, waiting for further instruction.

"Good girl," he told me, and those words rolled over me like an invisible caress. He sat down on the loveseat against the far wall and held his hand out to me. I moved quickly to take his hand, needing this more than I would have ever thought possible.

In no time I was face down over his strong thighs and his hand was running lightly over my upturned body, making me shudder with need. Suddenly I wanted those hands… those fingers slipping between my thighs and… I jerked with a gasp as the first swat pulled me from my mind's wanderings.

Another swat landed on the other cheek. "Ohhh."

"No more wandering, young lady, you stay with me right where we are," he told me. His hand began to fall faster and harder. Soon I couldn't hold still as the stinging heat began to cover my bottom.

Then he tilted me further over his knee and began to apply his hand with vigor to the tender crease where my bottom met my thigh and I could no longer hold back the tears. Harder and harder his hand fell, peppering each sit spot until I knew without a doubt I'd be sitting tenderly tomorrow. When his hand fell sharply three times in a row in the same spot, something inside me cracked wide open and I began to sob.

Suddenly I was cocooned against him in a warm embrace as he rocked me and rubbed my back, while I sobbed out all my heartache from broken promises and dreams.

"That's it, baby; let it all go… everything will be okay. I've got you," Eric crooned.

Finally, my well was dry and I felt completely empty.

Empty and alone, but then he tilted my tear-stained face up to his and kissed me, filling me up again.

His tongue devoured me, taking possession of everything in its path and I surrendered it all gladly to him. As we kissed, his hand smoothed down my stomach and between my legs.

I groaned as his knowing fingers sank into my wet heat, and I spread my thighs wide and begged for more, but he pulled away. I whimpered against his neck, the emptiness he left behind desperately needing to be filled.

He lifted me to my feet, and I began to shake. No, it couldn't be over... we couldn't be done!

"Silly girl," he said, pressing a kiss to my brow, leading me to the desk, and pushing me down over it with a hard swat to my still burning posterior. I heard his pants unzipping behind me and he moved in close, spreading my thighs apart and then teasing my weeping entrance with the head of his cock.

"Please..." I didn't care how needy I sounded as I begged and pushed back, trying to capture him with my body.

"Naughty girl," Eric said with a laugh, delivering ten more sharp swats that brought me up on my toes before cupping a burning ass cheek in each hand and spreading me impossibly wide. Then he was right where I needed him, his thick cock stretching my tender tissues around him as he pushed inside, filling my aching core to the hilt.

We both moaned at the exquisite feeling of our first joining as my body welcomed him. I was so slick with need he slid in smoothly despite my tightness. I felt my body clamp down on him as he moved to withdraw, as if it didn't want to let him go. I panted, the pleasure of his every movement drawing my muscles up like a wound rubber band, getting more and more taut with every stroke.

At first he gave just a few short shallow thrusts, then he pounded into me hard, the head of his cock bumping my cervix and snapping the rubber band. I came with a scream, shuddering beneath his still thrusting body.

Eric didn't pause in his masterful taking to let me catch my breath; instead he relentlessly pushed me over the hurdle of my first orgasm and straight into another and another. He rode me hard, taking complete possession of my body and making it his.

I clung helplessly onto the edge of the desk as he drove in and out of my quaking form. Letting go of my sore bottom, one hand snaked around my middle and down to cup my pulsing mound; sure fingers catching my throbbing clit and pinching it hard as he slammed into me hard one last time.

My back bowed and for a moment I lost my breath as my body shook with a powerful climax; spots danced before my eyes as everything in me clamped down and released again. He gave a shout of satisfaction and I felt his hot seed coat my inner walls, causing me to shiver again in response.

Nipping lightly as my shoulder and then kissing it before he pulled out, Eric patted my rump softly. "Good girl."

I could do nothing but slump over the desk; he'd left my body completely boneless. Fresh tears gathered in my eyes as I realized nothing would ever be the same again. It was as if with one dance, he'd completely torn me apart and remade me into something entirely new. I was no longer my own… I was his… his to keep or toss aside.

Then he gathered me in his arms once more and sat down on the couch with me in his lap, holding me close; he kissed the tears from my face then lifted my chin so I was drowning in chocolate once more.

"Don't cry, Anna, I've got you… you're safe here in my arms right where you belong," Eric said as my body relaxed against his, home at last.

CONSEQUENCES

"You will get the ginger and take fifty swats with the paddle with it still in and then fifty with the belt and we will finish with anal punishment," he said sternly.

Her bottom clenched almost reflexively at his words; this was going to be decidedly unpleasant. She'd known when she'd ignored his instructions not to masturbate as punishment the ante would be upped considerably, but Lily hadn't quite been prepared for what she was getting.

Her eyes moved to the ginger plug in his hand. Lily was very familiar with its stinging effect, but she'd never had it in during a spanking before, and she whimpered softly.

"Bedroom now." He pointed his finger, totally ignoring the beseeching look in her eyes. "Now, Lily."

The implacability in his tone sent her scurrying toward the bedroom with him close on her heels. She walked to the side of the bed and looked up at him; he just raised his brow expectantly.

Lily sighed and pulled her pants and panties completely off before bending over the end of the bed.

He was behind her almost instantly. "Spread your legs."

She buried her face in the bedding and moved her legs shoulder width apart as his hand spread her bottom cheeks open and she felt the cool tip of the root pressing against her ass determinedly.

"Deep breath, now let it out," he told her and as she exhaled, the ginger pushed all the way inside, making her gasp and go up on her toes.

He began firmly working it in and out of her bottom, much to her dismay. He increased his speed, taking her ass harder and harder with the ginger. "Ooohooo… ooooh," Lily cried as the burning began to fill the tender tissues of her ass.

"Do you like how this feels?" he asked.

"Noooo," she whined.

"No, sir," he corrected.

"No, sir!" Lily yelled after a particularly hard thrust.

"Are we going to have me time without permission again?" he asked.

"No, sir," she said softly. "Oww… owww… ooohooo." Lily couldn't stop the sounds as he continued filling her bottom ruthlessly, occasionally twisting the root inside her to increase the burn. Then finally he pushed it all the way in hard and left it there.

"You will count each ten," he instructed her.

The wooden paddle slapped hard against the underside of her bottom, the noise like a gunshot making her jump and clench around the intruder in her ass. Every time she clenched, more of the oils seeped into her bottom and made the burn worse. By the time the paddle had fallen ten times in a row, her bottom cheeks burned almost as badly as her asshole.

"Ten!" she cried.

He paused, and then began working the root again, much to her dismay. "Is all of this worth the behavior that earned it?"

"No, sir," Lily said miserably.

Then another ten swats were delivered with stinging accuracy. It soon became clear the ginger would be aggressively thrust in and out of her sore ass between each set of ten. By the time the last ten swats were delivered, she was sniffling softly into the mattress.

"Are you ready to be done with the ginger?" he asked.

"Yes, sir," Lily agreed eagerly.

In response he pressed it home harder than any of the previous times and twisted it one last time before removing it.

The burning sting inside her bottom stayed when the ginger left. She trembled when he picked up the belt. No time was wasted; line after line of fire was laid across her tender bottom until she'd gotten all fifty. The minute it was done, Lily collapsed over the side of the bed in relief.

It didn't last long.

Her breath caught when she heard the tell-tale sound of his zipper being lowered and his pants removed. "Get up in the center of the bed on your hands and knees."

Lily did as she was told with a shiver, trying to ignore the fact that throughout her punishment she'd grown increasingly wet. It was embarrassing the way her body responded to punishment.

She felt him move in behind her on the bed. "Legs apart."

Lily opened her legs again as he spread her wide and drove his cock into her ass with a forceful thrust.

"Ohhhhhh... owwww!" she yelled, as he pushed his way inside.

"Are you going to remember this?" he asked her as he took her hard and fast with no time for her tissues to prepare for the invasion.

"Yes, sir! I'll remember!" Lily said fervently as he rode her harder than ever before. It was weird; she loved anal, but this was different... it hurt, then for an instant there was a spark of the pleasure, then it hurt again.

The war between pleasure and pain seemed never-ending as he thoroughly reclaimed every part of her ass. As he thrust inside, he began to slap her bottom; she moaned half in pleasure and half in pain.

Finally, he pressed deep one last time and filled her ass with his seed. His body covered hers for a minute as he held himself deep inside her, his body wrapped around hers.

Then he pulled free, making her yelp. "Owww!"

"I bet," he told her. "Stay where you are." He returned quickly with a warm, wet cloth and gently cleaned her up before climbing back on the bed and holding her close.

"Do you think you can behave yourself?" he asked almost curiously.

"Yes, sir. I plan to be a very good girl, for a while anyway," Lily told him earnestly.

He snorted and kissed her head. "You better be."

Lily flipped over to face him in the bed. "You know, I've come to a decision."

"What's that?" he asked.

"Good girl anal is way better than bad girl anal," she said earnestly.

"It's supposed to be," he said with a grin.

"Bad girl anal is like, ooowww… ohooowww… hmmm… maybe… nope… owww!" Lily told him. "Good girl anal is like… I'm not sure… ooohhh… wow… oohooo yeah… harder please… oh yeah!"

He laughed. "Remember the feeling."

"Good girl anal all the way," she assured him.

He snorted—a little rudely, in her opinion, "We'll see."

STERN NERD IN THE PARKING GARAGE

Kelly caught her breath and sucked in her gut as he walked past; of course Mr. Stern-and-Nerdy-but-also-kinda-hot didn't even notice her.

She let out her breath in a disappointed huff, her belly pouched back out and her shoulders hunched. "Why do I bother?" Kelly asked the parking lot at large; no one answered but an extremely large pigeon that cooed rather excitedly her way.

Not really the type of male attention she'd been hoping for, though Mr. Pigeon continued to strut his stuff and look her way expectantly. What on earth did the pigeon think they had in common? Just then an equally excited coo sounded from right behind her and then a more dainty pigeon landed a few feet away from the male. He immediately puffed all his feathers out to appear even larger as he strutted around the female.

"Great, you weren't even talking to me! Rejected by a pigeon too! I'm really batting a thousand today!" she muttered as she walked back toward the offices.

"I beg your pardon?" a deep cultured voice spoke from directly behind her.

Kelly jumped with a little squeal, scattering several amorous pigeons that had joined their friends in the courting game and sending a spray of loose feathers around in their wake.

She turned to glare at no other than the hot nerd. "You scared me!"

"You scared the pigeons, after accusing one of them of rejecting you I believe. How did the pigeon reject you, pray tell?" he asked, cocking his head to one side and studying her like she was under a microscope.

"Like you care," she muttered under her breath.

"What was that?" he asked, stepping forward and reaching toward her.

Kelly gasped softly; was he making a move… did he find her attractive after all?

Then he pulled a feather from her hair and winked as he let it go to flutter to the ground. "Couldn't let you wander around with that in your hair; some of those birds have lice, you know."

"Bastard," she said sharply and then spun on her heel and stomped away.

"Stop right there, young lady!" His firm tone froze her in her tracks.

Kelly didn't quite know what to do; she didn't dare turn around and face the stern nerd who was now sending shivers up her spine and a flood of moisture into her panties. She felt him at her back, his body heat sinking into her; she tried not to react but was unable to suppress a shudder when his large hands fell on her shoulders.

He turned her bodily to face him, but Kelly refused to look higher than his throat.

"Look at me," he said firmly.

She shook her head, refusing to do as he asked.

"I said look at me." The implicit demand in his voice was difficult to ignore. Kelly found her head tilting slowly almost of its own volition and then his finger caught her beneath the chin and turned her face up to his. "I will now have an explanation for your behavior."

"I... and you... then... pigeons and you and..." was all she managed before tears filled her eyes and she began to cry, much to her embarrassment. So far in front of this man she'd been invisible, been caught talking to pigeons, and then called him a horrible name for no reason. He had to think she was a complete nutbar. That made her cry even harder, the thought that this beautiful man thought she was utterly crazy and therefore so out of his dating pool.

This was completely the most miserable moment of her life.

Then the unthinkable happened; Mr. Hot Sexy Stern Nerd cradled her against him and whispered soothingly to her as he began to rock back and forth until she calmed. Lord, but he smelled good; another gush of heat burst forth between her thighs, making her want to squeeze them together but she didn't want to be obvious.

Kelly shifted her legs slightly closer together, but then he tapped her bottom warningly. "Don't you dare."

"What?" She blinked her still tear-bright eyes up at him in confusion.

"You know what, young lady, pleasure later. First you and I have a few things to discuss," he said.

"We do?" Kelly asked in alarm, as a hot flush filled her face. He knew what she'd been doing... could this day get any worse?

"Indeed," he said sternly. "First I have a confession. I've been watching you for a few weeks and decided to ask you out today. I came back to do just that, but what do you suppose I found?"

Her eyes widened in alarm. "A woman going over lines for her part in a local play?"

He raised a brow at her. "Really?"

She sighed. "No, but it was worth a try."

"The list just gets longer," he said drily.

"List... there's a list?" Kelly asked.

"Indeed," he said.

"You say indeed a lot," she said, somewhat disgruntled. "What kind of list?"

"A list of infractions you will be punished for, of course," he said rather unsympathetically.

"Punished?" Kelly wished the word came out sounding sultrily sexy, but instead it came out in a squeak.

"So far I have cursing; it is really unseemly to call someone you barely know a bastard. Then there is lying, which I will never allow to go unpunished. Of course then we have the frightening of innocent pigeons; how exactly did you come to think a pigeon was coming on to you, by the way?" he asked curiously.

"I… er… well, I didn't really, but you had just rejected me and then the pigeon got all flirty but then I realized he wasn't flirting with me and it felt like rejection," she finished lamely.

"How on earth could I have rejected you when there was never an overture made?" he asked with a bit of outrage in his voice.

"I did my best sexy pose and you walked right on past!" Kelly yelled.

"Lower your voice. I did not walk right on past. I was coming back and found you being rejected by a pigeon."

"I didn't really think… this is a ridiculous conversation," she told him.

"I agree wholeheartedly. Shall I continue with my list?" he asked.

Kelly sighed; she rather liked being held in his arms and he still smelled good. "I suppose."

"Then there was the whole you feeling me up thing and trying to hump my leg," he told her.

"I did *not* try to hump your leg!" she yelled, mortified by the accusation. "I was merely trying to… well… I had this… ummm… ache."

"In your clit?" he asked knowingly.

Kelly gasped. "I… you can't… I… ooh… this is… I… I don't even know your name!" she finished her squeaked nonsense on a high note.

"It's Marc and that concludes my list. So yes or no, Kelly?" he asked, continuing to hold her close as he whispered the question again in her ear. "Yes or no?"

"Yes," she said softly, not even fully understanding what she was agreeing to. "Wait, how did you know my name?" she asked, looking up at him shyly.

"I told you I've been watching you for weeks. I asked around," Marc told her simply.

"Oh." Kelly blushed and focused back on his shirt button, picking at it nervously.

"Now about your behavior, young lady," he said sternly. "We will be discussing it further later."

"What do you mean, discussing it later?" Kelly asked, her bottom clenching reflexively.

"We'll be discussing it before I spank you, of course," Marc said matter-of-factly.

She nearly came at the word spank. It seemed her stern nerd was everything he appeared to be, in his sexy Clark Kent glasses. "I... ummm... oh my," was all she managed.

Marc grinned and tilted her face up to his again, only this time he pressed his lips lightly to hers in the whisper of a kiss... almost like a promise of kisses to come.

Then he turned her toward the building with a light swat on her bottom. "I'll see you after work right here. Don't be late."

· · · · · · ·

Kelly was there promptly at five when she got off work, and she frowned. She didn't see Marc; was it all a joke? How would he know spanking would be such a hot button for her? Was there something about her that gave a spanko alert?

"Sorry I'm late. I got caught up as I was leaving the office," Marc said from behind her, startling her and causing her to jump with a little scream again.

"Stop sneaking up on me!" she yelled at him, her hand still over her heart.

"Watch your tone, young lady, or I'll add it to my list," he told her.

"Again with the list," Kelly muttered.

"And so it's been added. I think we should go before you add any further infractions," Marc said, taking her firmly by the hand and pulling her toward his car.

"Hey, wait, ummm… shouldn't I follow you in my car?" she asked nervously.

"We aren't even leaving the parking lot yet. I think in this instance time is of the essence," he told her earnestly.

"Time is of the essence?" Kelly asked.

"Yes, I don't think I've ever met a woman in more dire need of a spanking."

"I'm not sure I would call it dire need," she said, not a little offended.

"I would," he said succinctly as he helped her into the back seat. The parking garage was almost completely deserted since it was after five on Friday, but she still looked around nervously.

Then she was over his knee with her skirt bunched up around her waist and panties at half-mast before she could blink. "I… ummm… you… my… oh, goodness…" There just weren't many ways to articulate *oh, my God… he's looking at my bare butt.*

Then his hand fell and all of her breath left her in a sharp hiss; man, that stung… more than expected.

His hand fell again and again, taking up a rhythm that only he could hear, but Kelly had no problem dancing to the beat, her bottom wriggling to and fro in an effort to escape his broad palm.

No matter how she moved, she never managed to evade his punishing hand. By the time he was finished, she was limp as a noodle, crying out her apologies as he rubbed a soothing hand across her inflamed backside.

"Are you going to be my good girl now?" he asked as his

hand stroked ever nearer her throbbing center.

"Yes, sir, I promise," she said with a sniff as she moved her thighs apart slightly. He rewarded her with the slick glide of his fingers across her needy clit before thrusting them deep inside. "Ohhhh… ohhhooo… please," Kelly panted.

The spanking had primed her for his touch; she spread her legs as far apart as the panties still around her knees would allow and he added a third finger, stretching her wide as his thumb played across her clit and she came completely undone.

"That's it, Kelly, come all over my hand like a good girl," he crooned to her as her inner muscles clamped down on his fingers and spasmed around them over and over. He continued to work them in and out as he stroked her clit, coaxing as much pleasure from her as possible.

Finally spent, she collapsed back over his knee with a breathy sigh. "Thank you, sir."

Marc flipped her in his arms and cuddled her close, kissing her forehead as she came back to earth. "You're more than welcome, baby. Are you ready to go to dinner now?"

Kelly blushed. "That's the first time I came before the date."

He chuckled and kissed her deeply. "It won't be the last," Marc said with a wink.

THE MUSIC'S LYRIC

Lyric smiled as she dropped her clothes at the edge of the wood with an excited shiver; the moon was high and it was time. She felt its glow warm her skin, every hair on her body standing up in response.

She hummed as she stretched her back sinuously, her long black hair flowing in luxurious waves to fall around her naked hips; her strange violet eyes lit with eager humor as she thought of the adventures she would have this night. Her people thought her strange with her coloring and light spirit, but her father understood. He said she was like her mother.

Lyric's mother had come from a far-off land, and she'd been what her father called Fae before he'd taken her, but she'd willingly embraced her wolf for him and she'd given him Lyric.

It had been during the birth of Lyric's younger brother that things had gone tragically wrong and somehow both of them—her mother and her infant brother—had been lost.

The loss had taken a toll on her father; he was often somber but occasionally his eyes would light on Lyric and a smile would fill them as he remembered. He was a good father, if a little overprotective, but he would let her run this night because there were no males in their wood that could take his little girl from him.

Lyric ran often, safe in their wood, where no male wolves had survived childbirth in almost twenty years. Generally the girls of her people took human mates from nearby villages, but she was nowhere near ready for such as that... she planned to enjoy her freedom as long as possible.

She enjoyed her lone travels through the woods of their mountain too much to give them up anytime soon.

Lyric felt the lick of heat run up her spine and embraced the change, bowing her back as muscle and bone popped, changing shape until she stood on all fours, a sleek black wolf with lavender eyes.

She gave one yipping howl toward home and then set off down the path and into the woods. The scents of other animals, rotten leaves, new grass and earth filled her senses as she ran. Easily skirting around trees and leaping fallen logs, she ran at full speed, opening herself up fully to the world around her and the pure joy of the run.

As she came bounding into the clearing to drink from the lake, she barely registered the slightly wrong scent before she was knocked to the ground.

She sat up and shook her head, moving to stand again when a low growl stopped her. Then she saw him: a huge black wolf far larger than herself standing over her, fierce amber eyes pinning her in place.

Before her eyes he changed, and a large man stood naked before her with the same startling amber eyes. "You do not ever bound into a clearing like that until you are told it is safe, little wolf."

Lyric narrowed her eyes and growled at him defiantly before rising to her feet.

He laughed at her. "Not used to rules, are you? Never fear, you will learn. Change," the man said firmly.

Lyric growled low in her throat again and turned to run back the way she'd come.

He caught her before she'd taken a step, holding her in

the air by the scruff of her neck like a pup.

"Now, little wolf, you will change and change now!" The power of his voice washed over her and Lyric found herself changing immediately, shifting while he still held her aloft. The man moved quickly, shifting his hold so he now held her up by her narrow waist.

He set her carefully on her feet in front of him, studying her naked form, from the top of her head to the tips of her toes. He eyed her full rose-tipped breasts, small waist, and full hips with the wealth of black curls swirling around them as she tried to shake off his thrall.

Lyric gave a small growl of protest, not liking the hold the stranger had on her or the way his muscular hair-covered physique made her feel. The strange heaviness in her breasts, the moisture building between her thighs as if he was… no! She would not have it!

"No!" she yelled up at him fiercely, her lavender eyes sparking with temper. "I will not have it! I will not have you!"

"Aye, but you will, little mate, you will indeed, but first I would have your name," he said firmly.

"I will not give it!" she spat.

"Your name." His voice deepened with the command and once again Lyric found herself helpless to resist.

"Lyric," she said, and then growled in frustration. "What do you do to me?"

"Oh, little Lyric, it is because you are mine, my destiny… my mate. I shall teach you to sing your pleasure for me," he said with a chuckle, the amber of his eyes swirling around into molten gold.

"No!" Lyric cried, her voice filled with a strange combination of passion and fear she didn't really understand.

"I am Daggen, and before we make music I must deal with your defiance, my pretty little mate, and teach you who is master here."

Before she could even think to dart away, he'd gone

down on one knee and pulled her face down over his leg, his hand falling hard and fast across her vulnerable bottom.

"Owww... no... you cannot do this! Owww... nooo!"

"I can, little mate, I can and am... you will learn to obey me and you will embrace me as your own," Daggen said firmly as his hand continued to fall.

Lyric whimpered as his hand continued to paint her bottom with fiery heat, stinging pain filling it while jolt after jolt of pleasure licked at her core. It was beyond understanding, this liquid heat that dripped freely from her slit while he spanked her like an errant child.

It was as if her body knew what he said was true and was preparing the way for him.

Suddenly the spanking ended and two long fingers slid into her pulsing sheath, making her cry out in pleasure.

"That's the music I wanted to hear, little one, sing for me," Daggen said as his fingers moved in and out of her, wringing cries of ecstasy from her lips until he pulled them free and set her on her knees.

Lyric whimpered in need and pressed her face to the ground, bringing her legs apart as she waved her bottom enticingly at her mate in a move as old as time. She needed him.

Then he was there... he filled her completely, stilling in a moment of perfect peace as they both absorbed the beauty of the moment of their joining.

She was his and he was hers.

Then he was moving inside her hard and fast, taking her, claiming her... leaving not one part of her body or soul untouched... but Lyric claimed him in return and soon both of their voices rose in a concert of pleasure and joy... as they made the music that was always destined to be theirs.

SKYLER

She took a deep breath and knocked on the door, her bottom already clenching reflexively. She was in big trouble… he'd promised her a thorough punishment to get his point across and her poor ass knew what was coming.

Jack opened the door and looked down at her, and her tummy flipped in response. "Skyler."

"Hi." She blushed when her voice squeaked.

For crying out loud, Skyler Jones, you're a forty-year-old woman. One frown shouldn't make you squeak like a fifteen-year-old caught with her daddy's cigarettes, she scolded herself internally as she ducked under Jack's arm and walked into the house.

"I don't think we need to talk about much, do we, little girl? Pretty much covered it the last time we talked, didn't we?" he asked.

Skyler fidgeted in front of him. "Yes, sir."

"Then I want you to strip," Jack commanded.

"Right now?" she asked, her face flushing deeply.

"Your heard me," he said sternly.

Her heart began to beat rapidly as her face grew more and more flushed; usually he waited till they were in the bedroom. "In the entrance hall?"

"Now, Skyler." His tone brooked no argument and

Skyler immediately pulled her panties and leggings off, then kicked her sandals away; as she did, her long shirt came over her head to join the pile. Under Jack's gaze, she unfastened her bra and tossed it with the rest of her clothes. It was embarrassing to be standing completely naked in his hall; she would have to walk through the living room past several open windows to get to the bedroom.

"Pick up your clothes and take them in the living room, while I get the ginger from the kitchen. I expect to find them neatly folded on the couch and you bent over the edge of the bed when I come out of the kitchen," Jack instructed as he walked through the living room to the kitchen.

Skyler moved swiftly, scooping up her clothes and standing in front of the couch and all the windows facing Jack's back yard as she neatly folded her clothing. She'd never felt so exposed in her life.

Once she was finished, she hurried to the bedroom and buried her face in his comforter; she was bent over the edge of his bed waiting for her punishment.

"Good girl," he said softly as he entered the room and she breathed a sigh of relief. Everything would be okay; Jack was going to punish her but she was still his good girl.

"Arch your back and spread those legs wide, little girl," he said firmly.

She did as he commanded and immediately felt the press of the big plug of ginger at the slick entrance of her vagina. "What?"

"I thought I'd lube it up for you first," he said and she could hear the grin in his voice. Then he sank it deep inside her and began working it in and out of her heated core.

Skyler moaned loudly as he rocked it in and out of her hard and fast; it felt good even as it began to burn. Just as her hips began to press back with every forward thrust, he pulled it free and pressed the now very slick root to her puckered anus.

"Deep breath and exhale," Jack told her as he began to work it inside her.

"Oooohhhh!" she cried, trying to make herself press back as it stretched her open and invaded her ass. Jack started the same in-and-out thrusts that had felt so good in her core and now made her go up on her toes in an effort to evade the evil little root.

But there was no chance she could escape it. It drove in and out of her ass hard and fast, making her whimper and moan as the burn began to grow, then he twisted it and seated it inside her.

"You know what to do," he told her.

Skyler stood and faced him with the root planted firmly then sank to the pillows in front of him on her knees while he unfastened his pants and pulled out his fully engorged cock.

She was equal parts desire and trepidation, embarrassed by the arousal slicking her thighs, as she leaned forward and took hold of his cock, licking all around the head.

"This isn't play time, suck me."

Engulfing the head of his cock in her mouth, Skyler began to suck hard while swirling her tongue beneath it. He allowed this for a minute, groaning his appreciation, then taking her hair firmly in his hands, he thrust hard into her mouth. She barely managed not to gag as he began to take her mouth hard, going deeper with every thrust.

When the head of his cock forced its way into her throat, she gagged reflexively, tears running from her eyes, but he held her fast, continuing to thrust when she would have pulled free. "Suck… suck… yes, that's what I want to feel… suck…"

He pulled all the way out just when she was at her limit. "Stroke me while you take a break and breathe… breathe, Skyler… deep breaths."

She took in a gasp of air in response to his command, breathing deeply as she squeezed his cock and worked her hand up and down it.

"Better?" he asked.

"Yes, sir," she said softly, feeling submissive to her core.

"Back on it then," he ordered. Skyler took him back in her mouth, sucking for all she was worth. This time, though he was thrusting just as hard, it seemed easier until he got close to coming. Then she started gagging again.

"Stay with it... keep sucking... I'm coming, stay on it!" He held her fast when she would have pulled away and she swallowed every drop as he came down her throat.

Skyler came off his cock gulping air, looking up at him as she caught her breath. "Lick me clean."

She leaned forward with a blush and licked every trace of cum from the head and his shaft then even licked all around his balls.

"Good girl, back in position."

Getting up from her knees, Skyler bent back over the edge of the bed. She groaned when he firmly grabbed the end of the ginger and began working it in and out of her again, twisting it periodically to increase the burn and the pressure in her ass.

"Are you going to be my good girl now?" Jack asked.

"Yes, sir... oooohooo... yes... please, I'll be good," she cried.

Once more he seated the plug, sending burning fire throughout her back passage, then she heard the sound of his belt clearing his pants.

The belt fell hard and fast on the under curve of her bottom, leaving a line a fire in its wake that rivaled the one inside her ass. Again and again it fell until not an inch of her backside was left untouched, as he worked the belt up and down her bottom and back up again.

Skyler cried softly into the bedding, then the belt dropped to the floor and the ginger was pulled almost all the way out and then thrust in again before it made its final exit.

"I'm sorry I was a bad girl," she said softly.

"I'm sure you are, Skyler. Now reach back and spread those ass cheeks wide for me," Jack told her.

With a little sniff, she did as he told her, catching a raw

ass cheek in each hand and spreading herself wide. It was mortifying; he could see everything from her wet glistening lips to her swollen tender asshole.

She gasped when she felt the press of his cock on that already sore orifice; she clenched involuntarily, but he would not be denied. "Ooohh, Jack!"

"What happens to naughty little girls, Skyler?" he asked as he pressed his cock deeper and deeper into her burning little hole.

"Naughty girls take it up the ass!" she yelled as he made it all the way inside and she felt his balls pressing tight against her ass.

"That's right, naughty girls get it up the ass hard," Jack told her as he began to thrust in and out of her ass in a punishing rhythm.

She moaned as she quickly became overwhelmed by the combination of pleasure and pain; Skyler frowned when he suddenly withdrew, disappointed by the loss of his cock.

"Flip over on your back," he said firmly.

Skyler flipped to her back, looking up at him curiously. "What?"

"I want to watch your face while I take your ass," he told her. Spreading her legs wide and pushing them back, he thrust back inside her tight bottom hole.

She gasped as he began pounding in and out once more, the new angle reawakening the sting as he stretched her tender hole open for his use.

"Spread your lips open for me," Jack ordered, after a particularly hard thrust.

Skyler blushed. "Why?"

"Don't ask me why, do as you're told or I'll spank those pretty lips bright red before I spank your naughty little clit," he told her matter-of-factly.

She reached down and spread her nether lips, holding them wide, feeling partly mortified at his unrestricted view and partly excited.

Then he snapped a tiny little paddle down on her clit and

her back arched as she yelped. He was still pounding in and out of her ass hard and fast and the combination of that with the clit spanking was overwhelming her senses.

"What do you say when I give you clear instructions, Skyler?" he asked as he delivered another stinging spank with the clit paddle.

"Yes, sir! I say yes, sir!" she cried as the little paddle fell again and again until she began to shiver as the pain morphed into some of the most intense pleasure she'd ever known.

Her body began to shake as he pounded into her even harder and continued raining spank after spank on her sensitive little nub until with a loud scream Skyler exploded, her anal muscles tightening down on his cock and milking it hard.

Jack followed her over the edge with a muffled shout, leaning down and sucking deeply on one of her nipples as he came.

His big body enveloped hers for a moment as they both came back down to earth. She loved the feel of him on top of her and around her; she felt safe and protected from the outside world.

Every time she shifted in her seat tomorrow with a wince, she'd remember this feeling and smile.

LETTING GO

Angie bit her lip as Brad secured her to the table. She'd told him she needed to let go completely… to give up all control.

He'd taken her at her word, commanding her to strip the minute she walked in the door. She'd shivered under the intensity of his gaze as she slowly removed all her clothing until she was standing naked and exposed before him.

Brad had taken her firmly by the elbow and bent her over the arm of the couch, pulling out a heavy tawse. "First I'm going to strap you until you let go of all the bad things that happened last week. You need this, don't you?"

Angie sighed as his hand rubbed lightly over her upturned bottom. "Yes, sir."

He stepped back to her side with one strong hand resting reassuringly in the small of her back. She heard a whoosh of air and then the tawse flattened her bottom all the way across, wrapping around as if hugging her ass before it lifted, leaving a wide line of fire in its wake.

Her back arched and she gasped just as it fell again, wringing a louder cry from her lips. Within five stripes every inch of her bottom was covered along with the top of her thighs. She whimpered as he worked his way back up her bottom, the heat and sting growing with every swat. The split ends of the tawse left a mean bite wherever they landed.

Angie lost count of how many times the strap fell before she finally collapsed in place over the arm of the couch, fully accepting the strapping would end when Brad was ready and not a moment before; tears of release and relief began leaking from her eyes.

She didn't even notice when the strap stopped falling.

"Good girl," Brad said as he rubbed the sore welted flesh of her bottom. "Better?"

She sniffled as she stood and buried her nose in his chest, sinking into him as he wrapped her in his arms.

He held her close for a moment then asked her if she was ready to continue.

"Yes, sir," Angie said softly, relaxing as she let herself embrace the submission of the moment and the peace that came from giving up control. No decisions to worry about; Brad would keep her safe… he would lead her through and bring her out the other side stronger.

Brad held out his hand and she placed hers trustingly in it, following him as he led her into the other room where he had a table set up. He patted the end of the table and she hopped up, giving a hissing little yelp when her well roasted bottom came in contact with the surface of it.

He chuckled. "Tender?"

"Yes," Angie said softly as he guided her to lie back on the table and he secured her arms above her head, stroking a finger down her side as he leaned down and caught an already tight nipple between his lips and sucked hard. "Ooooh…" she cried out at the exquisite feel of his mouth, the tugging sensation shooting straight to her throbbing clit as if attached by an invisible string.

He released her nipple with a pop and gave the other one the same treatment, leaving her panting and whimpering by the time he finished. She watched him, both nipples throbbing in time with the pulse in her clit as he attached a spreader bar to her ankles and then giving a little gasp of surprise when he lifted the bar and attached it to a hook in the ceiling, her feet wide apart just above her face.

She was fully exposed to anything he wanted to do to her, unable to move at all. She could do nothing but take what he gave her, be it pleasure or pain.

"You okay, little girl?" he asked, rubbing a gentle circle on her tummy.

A tension Angie hadn't realized she was holding relaxed and she smiled at him. "Yes, sir."

"Good girl," Brad said as he began moving something up on rollers. She frowned and tried to see what it was but was unable to see, then she felt the press of a large dildo stretching her as it was pushed slowly inside.

"Oooh… that's really big…" she cried as it continued to stretch her slick channel open with its girth and seemingly unending length.

"You can take it," he assured her as he began working it in and out of her until she was begging him to give it to her harder. In response he delivered two sharp swats to each already burning bottom cheek. "Who's in charge here?"

"You," Angie said breathlessly.

"That's right. You have no control here… maybe this will help you remember that," Brad said as he brought another dildo, this one more slender, to the little pucker of her ass.

"Ooohooo," she gasped as he worked the well lubed phallus in just as thoroughly as he had the first one. She felt stuffed full in both holes by the time both dildos were seated to his satisfaction. A whirring sound filled the air and then both of the cocks started moving in tandem, slowly rocking out of her and then sliding back in again.

The sensation of having both holes taken so thoroughly at the same time was indescribable, the pleasure almost too intense; then she felt Brad bending over her and when he sucked her swollen clit into his mouth, she came immediately with a scream.

"There's my girl," he said with a grin, standing and

smiling down at her with her essence still glistening on his lips. He picked up a strange little suction cup and then placed it over her clit, seating it perfectly in place before turning it on.

"Ooohhooo…" Her back bowed as she cried out; the little thing was vibrating and sucking her clit as the dildos planted deep inside her began moving harder and faster. "I can't…" Angie gasped.

"You can and you will," Brad told her sternly as he began to slap her exposed bottom cheeks, reawakening the sting. "Come now!"

She came screaming his name, not getting the chance to come down from the intense orgasm before the machine worked her back up the peak and shot her into another.

Angie was lost in a sea of sensation so pleasurable it was almost painful as he altered the patterns of the machine again and again… forcing orgasm after orgasm from her shuddering body.

He stayed with her the whole time, occasionally petting her or sucking her nipples as she came… sometimes he commanded her to orgasm and other times scolded her, reminding her she had no control over her body when she protested.

By the time it was over she was crying tears of release with every orgasm and she was almost drunk with pleasure; her whole body was flushed and sensitive. She had another little orgasm when he removed the dildos and the suction device from her clit.

When he released her from her restraints and lifted her from the table, Angie realized her legs were like limp noodles, she was so completely spent. Brad chuckled again and scooped her high in his arms, carrying her into the bathroom and sitting her in the warm tub.

Angie sighed in pleasure as he gently washed and dried her before putting her in the bed and climbing in behind her. Wrapping her tightly in his arms, he kissed her shoulder.

"Was it everything you hoped for?" he asked.

Angie sighed, turning her head to kiss the hand beneath her cheek. "It was everything and more. Thank you," she said with a sigh as she drifted off into a dreamless sleep, freed from all her burdens and cares.

YOURS

Naked on my knees in front of you... my body pressed against your legs... I can feel your rigid cock between my breasts; suddenly I'm hungry for the taste of you. My nose nuzzles into the waistband of your jeans as my tongue darts out to lick lightly just below your belly button.

A firm hand jerks my collar as you catch me beneath the chin with your other hand and tilt my head back. "Good girls don't just grab what they want, they ask politely."

I shudder softly at your stern words, wanting to please you. I'd known better than to touch without asking.

"I'm sorry, Daddy. May I please suck your cock?" I look up at you from my position with my head still held firmly back.

You smile and slid your thumb into my mouth. I suck on it eagerly, flicking my tongue around it at the same time.

"Does my baby girl need something bigger to suck on?" you ask with a smile.

Your thumb slides out of my mouth, rubbing my own saliva on my lips; the friction of the pad of your thumb gliding across them gives me a shiver of pleasure. "Yes, please."

"What a good girl, asking so politely and then waiting

patiently." You release me from your hold and I watch as you undo the snap of your jeans and the zipper slowly.

Then your beautiful cock springs free, so long and thick… a pearly drop of pre-cum leaking from the little slit in the head. I lick my lips, suddenly needing you as much as I need my next breath.

You step back from me to kick your pants and underwear to the side and then you're back pressing against the front of my body; the hair on your legs tickles my nipples, causing me to arch my back and rub against you like the kitten you sometimes call me.

I rub my face against your cock, nuzzling against it. My hands rest on your legs as I begin to lick lightly at the base of your shaft and balls before ghosting my tongue up the length of your cock.

As I get to the weeping tip, a soft moan escapes me as I catch the little drops of pre-cum on my tongue. I love the taste, the smell of you; it's like your very essence wraps around me in a cape of need.

My hands softly squeeze your thighs as I catch the large head of your cock in my mouth; my tongue swirls around beneath it as I begin to suck, enjoying the feel of you in my mouth.

Your hands come to rest in the hair on either side of my head, letting me stay where I am for a moment, then your hands tighten.

"Take me deep," you rasp hoarsely.

I open my throat to you as your hands slip down to grasp each side of my collar and you begin to thrust inside. I continue to suck and lick as you move in and out of my mouth, arching my neck a little to ease your way down my throat.

Your deep moan fuels my own need for everything you have to give. I increase the suction, bobbing my head up and down in time with your thrusts and starting to swallow and work my throat around your pulsing cock.

Your hands in my collar tighten and you begin to pump

harder. I gag a little as you begin to take my mouth a little rougher; the muscles in your thighs tighten and I know you're about to come. I stop sucking and just relax my mouth around you as you begin to fill my mouth with stream after stream of cum.

I swallow everything you give me, smiling softly around you as you tell me what a good girl I am. As your body relaxes, I begin to gently lick you clean so there isn't a drop of you wasted.

You pull gently away to sit down in your big chair; I crawl into my place between your knees and rest my head on your leg.

"That's my sweet baby girl." Your hand begins to softly caress my head and hair as we sit quietly together. I am awash in your pleasure, content for the moment to simply belong.

THE GLASSCLOCK COUNTY FAIR

"Are you completely insane?"

Emma jumped when the strident exclamation was voiced directly behind her, almost losing her balance on the stepladder she was precariously balanced on. "Good night Irene, Jen! You almost gave me a heart attack!" she said, frowning as she adjusted the angle of the sun catcher mobile she was hanging in the doorway of the big white tent.

"You should be so lucky! Do you have any idea what kind of punishment you're bringing down on yourself when Will sees this?" Jen asked, dramatically waving her hands around to encompass the merchandise neatly arranged around the tent's interior.

Emma smiled. "Don't be silly." She thought fondly of her boyfriend as she critically studied the array of glass dildos varying in size from small to extremely large. Grinning at her friend, she ran a hand lightly along the mobile, making the tiny, multi-colored glass dicks sway in the breeze; different colors refracting from the sun falling on the little sun catchers displayed cheerily on the white inner walls of the canvas tent. "Isn't that pretty?"

"Have you even met my brother?" Jen asked incredulously. "There is no way he knew this was what you meant when you said a souvenir tent."

"What could be more fitting for a souvenir tent for the Glasscock County Fair than... well, glass cocks?" Emma asked with her hands on her hips. "I'm sure Will won't mind at all."

"He'll not mind all over your backside!" Jen declared.

Emma rolled her eyes in the earnest young woman's direction, ignoring the little flutter of alarm low in her belly. Surely Will wouldn't take exception to her booth. He certainly wouldn't spank her, would he? Will was the chief of police in Garden City, the county seat of Glasscock County. They'd met shortly after she moved to town when he pulled her over for speeding. The next night they'd gone out to dinner and had been together ever since.

She shivered as she remembered the next time he'd pulled her car over and given her a ticket. Will had also pulled her over his knee and given her a quick version of what he called Texas justice by paddling her tail bright red. Emma chewed her lower lip, but that was for speeding... her souvenir booth was something entirely different.

"I'm sure everything will be fine. Don't you think everyone will see the humor of my little booth?"

"How can you even ask such a question? Do you know the women that run the Glasscock County Heritage Foundation County Fair committee?" Jen asked in horror. "These women are not the glass-dildo-sun-catcher-penis types. You do realize you live in one of the most conservative counties in Texas now, don't you?"

"It's not like I moved here from the moon, for goodness' sake. Jennifer, you are really overreacting," Emma tried to reassure her friend.

Then there was a gasp from directly behind them. "Oh, my sweet lord!"

Geneva Hildebrande, this year's chair for the Heritage Foundation County Fair committee stood there aghast; her face was bright red as she stared at the garishly colored mobile of colored glass phalluses.

"Hi, Ms. Hildebrande," Emma said cheerfully.

The woman fixed Emma with a glare. "This is not what the committee had in mind when you said souvenirs, young lady."

Emma's ready smile began to falter as she realized Jen was right. Her little souvenir booth was not going to be well received.

"Unacceptable." Emma and Jen watched as the woman whipped out her cell phone and began to dial. "Sheriff, I need you to get out to booth 27A immediately; we have a problem that needs to be dealt with posthaste."

Snapping the connection closed, the old battle ax fixed Emma with a glare. "You wait right here, young lady. The sheriff will get to the bottom of this."

"What seems to be the problem, Geneva? I was busy over there sampling the fried food and… well, I'll be a monkey's uncle!" Sheriff Ellis stopped in his tracks, seemingly entranced by the brightly colored glass cocks sparkling in the bright sunlight. Clearing his throat, he came back to himself with a shake of his head. "I see… well, Geneva, I'm afraid since the fairgrounds are within the Garden City Limits, this isn't my jurisdiction."

"What do you mean, not your jurisdiction? Something has to be done about this!" the woman exclaimed. "The fair opens tomorrow! Children will be present!"

Emma winced; she hadn't really thought about kids. She'd never really been around any and tended to forget all about them.

The sheriff pulled out his own phone. "Don't worry, Geneva. Yes, chief, we got us a situation over here at the fairgrounds. Booth 27A, yes, it's Emma's booth all right. Well, sir, she's got herself a bunch of glass peckers laid out all over the place. Not a very seemly booth for a young lady to run iffen you ask me." The sheriff winced and pulled the phone away from his ear as the chief began to yell.

Emma was glad she wasn't close enough to hear what Will was yelling.

"I'll do that. See you in a minute." Sheriff Ellis hung up and pinned Emma in place with a stern frown. "The chief said you were to wait right here."

She gulped nervously.

Next to her Jen smirked and mouthed a quick, "I told you so."

Then Bubba Hildebrande chose that moment to walk up next to his mother. "Well, I'll be flipped. Are those colored tally-whackers hanging from that there mobile?"

"Bubba, please! You're in mixed company!" Geneva barked.

The forty-year-old man blushed. "Sorry, Mama."

Emma was mortified; her good idea was obviously up in smoke. She had to live in this town. Would these people be able to get past her gross error in judgment? She just wanted to escape, preferably before Will got there.

She began to subtly inch her way out of the tent doorway toward where her van was parked when a large hand clamped down on the back of her neck. "I don't think so, young lady. There will be no running from the scene of the crime."

Emma glanced up into the angry face of her captor. "Hi, honey."

"What in the hell were you thinking, Emma?" Will asked her.

"Well, it is Glasscock County and I thought..." She stopped as Will and everyone else around her watched disapprovingly. Emma's shoulders slumped; explanations didn't matter, her goose was cooked. "I'm sorry."

"Not yet, but believe me, baby, you will be," Will whispered in her ear before he began to direct several deputies and police officers to pack up her tent. Emma was sent to wait in her van, a sharp slap to the seat of her jeans sending her on her way.

Terribly embarrassed but glad to be out from under everyone's censorious gaze, she sat in the driver's seat with her forehead resting on the steering wheel. She decided to use the ostrich approach to the situation; if she couldn't see it, it wasn't happening.

• • • • • • •

Will looked over at the slumped figure in the van and shook his head. He had no idea what got into Emma sometimes.

"You sure got yourself a pistol in that girl, Will," the sheriff said with a grin as he clapped him on the back.

"You have no idea, Glen," Will said as his eye caught the glittering glass mobile and wondered who in the hell would buy such a thing. A slow smile spread across his face as he had an idea.

Grabbing one of the sacks Emma had set aside for purchases, he dropped the garishly inappropriate sun catcher inside along with one fairly large glass dildo and one of a more modest size, as well as a couple of glass butt plugs. As he'd studied her wares, Will decided it would be best if the punishment fit the crime.

Little Miss Emma was about to experience the difference between Glasscock County and an actual glass cock up close and personal.

"Can you boys get the rest of this stuff to Emma's garage? I have a little matter that needs my immediate attention," Will asked the sheriff and the rest of the officers.

They all nodded they were good; some with knowing smirks and a few actually snorted and gave him a thumbs up. Most of the men in this part of Texas still felt the application of their palm to a naughty female bottom went a long way toward keeping the home harmonious. Will was no exception.

Gathering his bag and hat, Will went to help Emma from her van to his squad car.

"You're arresting me?" she asked in alarm.

"Nope," was all he said.

"Ummm… where are you taking me?" Emma asked.

"My house," Will said succinctly.

"What's happening at your house?" The question came out in an unnaturally high voice.

Will looked at her with one arched brow. "I think you know."

Emma turned bright red and began to fidget nervously in her seat. "Will, can we talk about this? I didn't mean to do anything wrong... I just... I thought it would be a fun booth... and... I... well... upon reflection I might not have thought things completely through but..."

"Might not have thought things completely through?" he asked incredulously.

"I'm sorry!" she squeaked.

"I can assure you that you will be one very sorry little girl before it's all said and done."

"What are you going to do?" she asked again, her alarm only growing when he pulled to a stop in his driveway.

"First you're going straight in that house and then you're going to take off all your clothes," he said matter-of-factly while Emma shook her head.

"No... I can't do that!" She grabbed the front of her shirt as if to ward off even the thought.

"Don't tell me no, young lady, you will go in that house and do exactly what I said unless you want me to go out back and cut a switch to use on top of everything else you've already earned," Will said ominously.

"You're going to spank me?" Emma asked hoarsely, her back pressed against the passenger door.

"You bet your soon to be hot little bottom. First I'm going to take you over my knee and give you a good hard spanking. Then you and I are going to investigate some of your glass cocks very carefully while you bend over the end of my couch and then you're going to make the acquaintance of my belt," Will informed her, raising a brow once more. "Any questions?"

Eyes as wide as saucers, Emma shook her head before stammering, "N-n-no, sir."

"Then get your ass in that house and strip. I expect to find you with your nose in a corner, unless you really do want me to cut that switch," he barked.

She nearly fell out of the car in her haste to get the door open and run inside. Will followed at a much more leisurely pace. He wanted to give his naughty girl time to stew in her own juices a little before he delivered her punishment.

He was pleased to walk into the living room and find a very naked Emma with her face pressed tightly into the corner waiting for him. As she heard him enter, she seemed to try to cram even more of herself into the corner.

Will smiled to himself as he grabbed some fishing line out of a drawer and used it to hang the ridiculous glass mobile from the ceiling fan low enough that it would be at eye level for Emma, both when she was over his knee and bent over the arm of the couch. He wanted it to be in her line of vision throughout the phases of her punishment.

Then he pulled his police belt from around his lean hips; laying his gun holster down on the bar and folding the thick leather belt in half, he left it on the coffee table in easy reach.

When he removed both the glass cocks from their boxes and laid them next to the belt, he noticed one of them came with warming lube. As he read more about the lube he grinned; the lube heated itself upon contact with the skin and the heat level increased with friction. That was fortuitous indeed.

Will rolled up his shirtsleeves as he sat down on one end of the couch; he was ready. "Come here, Emma."

She turned to face him with a whimper, eyeing him nervously.

Will drank in the sight of her naked body; the nipples on her full breasts were already tight with need. Their rosy tips looked like ripe berries begging to be tasted. He had to drag himself away from that thought; there were other things that needed to be handled first.

He held out a hand to her. "Emma?"

Will saw her look from him to the items resting on the

coffee table before coming back to rest on him as she licked her lips. "Honey, can we talk about this?"

He raised a brow. "Are you unclear about why you're being punished?"

"Not exactly…" she hedged.

"Come here, Emma. Don't make me tell you again." This time he said it with just enough bite and she came forward to stand in front of him in a breathless rush of energy.

Grasping her firmly by the arm, Will pulled her down over his lap, leaving her bottom raised high for punishment.

· · · · · · ·

Emma groaned as Will shifted her around on his lap until he had apparently found the perfect position to roast her hind end. Mortified by the whole situation and embarrassingly aware of how wet she was at the thought of both the spanking and the glass cocks resting so innocently on the coffee table, she pressed her face into the couch.

Her head sprang back up with a cry of dismay when his hard palm clapped off her naked bottom with a loud slap. "Owwwwww!"

"You will keep your head up and look at that godawful mobile of glass penises while I spank you. I want you to remember exactly what brought you to be over my knee getting your bare bottom spanked like a naughty little girl," he said as another hard slap fell.

Emma groaned, suddenly embarrassed by the site of the garish glass mobile. What had she been thinking?

The twinkling colors sparkling in the light from a nearby window seemed to mock her as Will's hand fell again and again until Emma couldn't really focus on anything but the heat rapidly building in her posterior.

Surely the spanking had to be over soon, she thought desperately; he'd covered every inch of her poor bottom at least five times. Then he tilted her further over his knee and locked her legs between his.

"Warm-up's over," he said succinctly.

Then his hand fell on the tender crease where her bottom met her thigh and she realized she'd only thought he'd been spanking hard before. When his hand began to fall repeatedly in the exact same spot, she began to wail.

"Please, Will! I'm sorrrreeeee! Ohhhhhhh…. owwwww… oooohhh, that spot's done! It's done, I tell you!" she cried frantically. She breathed a sigh of relief at first when he moved to the other side but soon Emma found herself trying to buck and twist off his knee in an effort to escape his punishing palm.

On and on Will spanked until finally with a sob Emma collapsed over his knee, giving herself over to his punishment.

As if a sign of submission was all he'd been looking for, the spanking ended and Will lightly stroked a hand over her tender flesh.

"That part's over, baby, now get up and bend over the end of the couch for me." He helped Emma to her feet and guided her into place over the arm of the couch. She cringed when he made her spread her legs wide, knowing everything was on display to him from the wetness seeping from her needy sheath to the tight little rosebud of her ass.

She watched out of the corner of her eye as he picked up the glass butt plug; thankfully, while it wasn't the smallest she'd ordered, it wasn't the largest either. A flush of heat filled her face and neck as she watched him coat it in the heating lube.

Emma knew she'd never be able to look at a glass penis without blushing again and she wasn't positive she'd ever be able to even say the county name out loud again. She'd certainly never poke fun at it again!

"Spread your bottom cheeks open wide for me, Emma," Will instructed her.

She obediently caught a sore cheek in each hand, wincing as she pulled them open wide; Emma was so wet she knew she had to be dripping on the floor. Half of her was afraid, but the other half... the other half wanted everything Will was doing and more. She shivered and buried her face in the couch cushion.

A gasp escaped her at the first feel of the cool slippery glass pressing against her most private place.

"Try to relax your bottom and press back to meet me, baby, it won't hurt as bad that way."

Emma did her best to relax as she pushed back, whimpering a little as the broad head of the plug pressed against the tender ring of muscle guarding her secrets. Then with a burning sensation the muscles gave way and it popped inside, forcing her little hole to stretch open around it.

She groaned as Will moved it in and out of her, seating it a little further inside with every thrust until it was all the way in and she felt full, but at the same time aware of the aching emptiness of her pulsing channel.

"Good girl," Will praised her, stroking a hand down her back before moving on to the next item on his agenda.

As she watched him pick up the large glass dildo, Emma's vagina clenched in anticipation; he was about to fill the place that was aching with need. She was so wet no lube was needed and Will was able to slide the glass phallus inside her to the hilt.

Emma moaned loudly; she felt impossibly full with both glass phalluses resting inside her so deeply. She moved restlessly over the arm of the couch, wanting... needing Will to move them inside her.

"Now, young lady, do you still think selling glass cocks at the Glasscock County Fair is a funny idea?" Will asked her sternly.

"No, sir!" she answered earnestly.

"What about glass dildos? Are they a laughing matter?" he asked as he began moving the two seated inside his naughty girl in and out of her in tandem.

Emma helplessly rocked to and fro with each thrusting

movement inside her; the glass cock stretching her ass was getting hotter and hotter with every stroke. Her ass was on fire inside and out, making her impossibly wet.

A hard slap startled her. "I asked you a question, young lady."

"No, sir, glass cocks are not a laughing matter," she said in a husky voice that ended in a soft wail when he lightly pinched her clit. He continued to tease the swollen bud as he alternately moved each of the glass dildos until every muscle in Emma's body tightened down preparing for an intense climax. "Will… I'm going to come so hard…" she panted.

He chuckled and stopped everything. "Not yet you're not."

Emma could have cried; every nerve in her body was thrumming with intense arousal and aching need. She'd never been this worked up in her life. It felt like if she didn't come soon she'd die. The ache was so intense… and the burning heat filling her ass had morphed from discomfort into mix of pleasure and pain indescribable in its intensity.

Both of the phalluses were thrust back inside her as deep as they would go before Will patted her bottom and stepped away.

"I'm going to give you ten with the belt, Emma; you stay in position or I'll start over," he told her as he placed one strong hand in the center of her back to help her stay in place.

Emma shivered, taking comfort in the feel of his broad hand on the small of her back. She heard the whistling sound of the belt just before it caught her on the under curve of her bottom, leaving a line of fire in its wake and jolting both the glass dildos inside her.

Emma panted through the pain and the wave of pleasure that followed closely on its heels. Will wasted no time bringing the belt down again and again. Emma found herself humping her bottom up and down, unsure whether she was reaching for another stroke of the belt or trying to escape it; each stroke bringing her closer to the orgasm waiting just out of her reach.

She was caught up in a world somewhere between pleasure and pain; afraid the belt would never stop falling but a part of her deep inside never wanted it to end. The last stroke fell hard, lifting her up on her toes with a keening cry as tears glistened on her cheeks.

Then Will pulled the glass phallus from her ass. Emma whimpered at its loss, feeling bereft. When the broad head of Will's cock pressed against the sore opening of her ass, she almost wept with relief as she pressed back to welcome him inside.

He slid in to the hilt easily; she groaned as his thighs slapped against her sore bottom, awakening the sting. Emma moved her legs further apart as he began to ride her hard, one hand coming around to work the glass cock inside her dripping canal, his thumb hitting her clit with every inward stroke.

The first orgasm slammed into her brutally, bowing her back with pleasure as she tightened around him and shuddered beneath him. Will didn't give her any respite, continuing to move without pause and hurtling her straight into another orgasm so intense she saw spots in front of her eyes.

This time when her body clamped down around him and began milking him, Will shouted hoarsely and buried his face against her as she felt the heat of his seed bathe the inside of her ass.

Will gently pulled away from her and removed the glass phallus inside her still pulsing sheath. Emma groaned and shivered as he pulled it free from her body before lifting her high in his arms.

She snuggled into his chest as he carried her to the bathroom and cleaned them both up. When he settled her in the bed and wrapped himself around her, Will pressed a tender kiss to the top of her head.

"I love you, Emma."

"I love you too, Will."

"No more glass cocks?" he asked, smiling against the back of her neck.

"No more glass cocks," Emma assured him quickly. "I'll sell them on eBay."

"We'll keep the ones we used and I picked a couple more out just in case," Will told her.

"In case of what?" Emma asked in nervous anticipation.

"You never know what could happen in Glasscock County."

BOOBTASTROPHE AT THE
GLASSCOCK COUNTY FAIR

Virgie eyed her full figure critically in the mirror then relaxed with a smile; while she wasn't entirely comfortable in her own skin, Earl loved her curves and was sure to like what he saw. The sweetheart neckline of her long lavender t-shirt exposed a good amount of cleavage, her bountiful breasts plumping out in a rather tempting display. Her new jeans were much snugger than she normally wore and cupped her full bottom like a lover.

Her makeup was a little heavier than normal but she was going for the pin-up girl look; the heavy kohl liner and smoky accents made her hazel eyes pop and the red lipstick emphasized her lips. She'd piled her curly red locks on top of her head in artful disarray with a lavender scarf tied loosely beneath the curls. Her look was finished off with low-heeled sandals and bright red toenails.

Virgie felt pretty... sexy... ready to tackle the world, or at the very least Earl.

She smiled at her reflection when the doorbell rang and hurried to answer his summons. The door swung open and she stepped back with her hands on her hips and grinned up at him. "What do you think?"

"I think you're showing a lot of cleavage, little girl," he said with a frown.

"What?" Her chin quivered as she realized he was less than pleased; this reaction was not what she'd expected. "I thought you liked my curves." Her shoulders slumped and she wrapped her arms over her chest to cover the area he'd spoken of, how embarrassing…

"Oh, don't look like that, baby, I do like your curves, in fact I love them… but I don't like the idea of every other fella in town eyeing my real estate."

"You think I look fat!" she wailed, as one big tear trickled down her cheek.

"Virginia Elizabeth, did I say you were fat?" The sudden stern tone in Earl's voice brought her up short.

She sniffled. "Not exactly."

"I beg your pardon?" This time Earl's arms were crossed over his chest and he lifted one eyebrow at her with a stern frown.

Virgie squirmed from foot to foot for a minute before answering glumly, "No… you didn't call me fat, but I thought you'd think I looked pretty… I worked so hard to be pretty for you and now it's all ruined!"

Earl laughed. "You do look pretty, darlin' and nothing is ruined. Are you sure that top is gonna stay put and nothing is going to pop out?" he asked as he dubiously eyed the sweetheart neckline of her pretty shirt.

She laughed and waved off his concerns. "Don't be silly, Earl! The girls will stay right where they are; women wear sweetheart necklines all the time with no issue."

Hurrying to the car, she wondered if Earl would insist upon driving five miles under the speed limit as usual. Virgie adored the man but sometimes he was a bit of a fuddy-duddy.

The Glasscock County Fair was the event of the year in Glasscock County, Texas, at least in Garden City it was. Virgie looked forward to it every year. She liked to find out who had what booth and who won the pie contest and the best preserves.

She'd heard the chief of police's new girlfriend caused quite a stir with her glass cock booth at the beginning of the fair. It had of course been quickly shut down. Virgie was actually sorry she'd missed that little show. Thinking about all the goings-on in Glasscock County, she grew more eager to get to the fair and was sitting on the edge of her seat. There was sure to be some juicy gossip she hadn't already heard regarding what was now known as the glass cock incident. Virgie had heard there had even been a sun catcher mobile covered in colorful little glass peckers.

"Sit back in your seat, young lady, and fasten your seatbelt," Earl said firmly. "Sitting forward won't make the car go any faster."

Virgie blushed and sat back, fastening her seatbelt into place. Earl was a bit of stickler for societal rules. Rules she forgot sometimes in her excitement to be somewhere, but her man had no problem reminding her, sometimes really hard on her bare bottom.

She grinned as they pulled into the fairgrounds and parked. "What do you want to do first, Earl?"

He smiled down at her rather indulgently; she knew it was easy to get caught up in her excitement, as she was such an exuberant little thing. Sometimes he reined her in hard, but she tried to be his good girl. "How 'bout we start on the midway then make our way over to the rides?"

She normally stayed away from the rides, but Earl enjoyed rides so she knew she'd let him persuade her onto some of the tamer ones. "Okay, honey."

By the time they left the midway, Virgie was carrying a huge white and pink stuffed unicorn with a golden horn to the amusement of everyone they walked past.

They were having a wonderful time and everything was going great until they got on the Graviton. It was a big circular cage with back rests that you stood against and a metal chain across your middle to hold you in place.

Earl fastened her belt across her midsection then took

his place next to her and fastened his own. They grinned at each other as the ride started spinning. Then they had to rest their heads back as it got faster and faster.

Soon everyone was laughing hysterically. Virgie felt a giggle build in her own throat in response… it never occurred to her she might be the reason for the laughter.

"Hey, lady! You're gonna choke yourself!" a young male voice yelled from the other side of the circle about the same time Virgie realized her upper chest area was getting chilled. She looked down and gasped in alarm.

Her girls were about to break free from their bonds. The antigravity force of the Graviton had already lifted them to the point they were swelling above her sweetheart neckline and almost in her throat.

Just at the moment her bra lost its ability to contain disaster, Earl finally realized what the kids were laughing about and looked at her. Her boobs had burst forth in all their glory.

"Virginia Elizabeth!" Earl exclaimed when her girls made themselves completely known to one and all. He vainly tried to cover them with his cowboy hat as the ride continued to spin but his Stetson just didn't have the capacity to contain his girl's bountiful breasts.

Virgie was completely mortified and tried to cover what Earl's hat missed with her arms, but the constant motion of the ride made her dizzy and wobbly, so every time she had them somewhat under wraps her arms flung open, releasing them again and knocking Earl's hat away to free her runaway boobs once more. It was a vicious cycle and from the muscle she saw ticking in her man's jaw out of the corner of her eye, it was a cycle that was going to viciously bite her in the ass.

Finally the ride ended and before she could even attempt to, Earl was shoving her boobs back into her bra and tugging her sweetheart neckline as high as he could. "Women have been wearing sweetheart necklines for years," he mimicked in a falsetto voice, making her wince.

"Honey, in my defense, I had no idea of the kind of effect an antigravity ride would have on my H cups. It just never occurred to me. Really, when you think about it, they should have some sort of warning sign."

"I'll be flipped. Mama, did you see that? Virgie's titties were flying all over the place. What a fair this turned out to be... first all them glass tally-whackers and now Virgie's tits!" The sound of Bubba Hildebrande's running commentary was probably the death knell for her backside.

"Bubba! We do not say titties or tits... they are breasts! And I told you I never wanted to hear that other word again!" Ms. Hildebrande told her son sharply.

"Yes, Mama," Bubba said dutifully while watching Earl and Virgie approach. "Hey, Earl, Virgie, you're looking mighty fine tonight."

Virgie suppressed a shudder at Bubba's leer then looked up and saw Ms. Hildebrande eying her with distaste as Earl hustled her past. *Probably wants me charged with public lewdness, the old cow!*

A sharp swat landed on the seat of her tight bottom-hugging jeans, jolting her to the side as Earl grabbed her arm. "Virginia Elizabeth, apologize this instant!"

Crap, she'd said that last bit out loud; flushing, she smiled as sweetly as she could at the cow in question. "I'm terribly sorry for my rudeness and my public display, Ms. Hildebrande."

"Mmmmm," was all the old bat said before turning her back and grabbing her still leering son by the ear to lead him away. Sometimes Virgie felt a little sorry for Bubba; after all he was the same age as her, not four.

"Mama!" Bubba complained as his mother continued to lead him away while delivering a blistering tirade about his behavior and fast women.

Virgie glared; she was hardly a fast woman. "Poor Bubba."

"You'd do better to worry about poor Virgie," Earl told her sternly. "Wait here."

She stood obediently by one of the ticket booths while Earl returned to the scene of the crime to retrieve her unicorn. It made her smile that he'd thought of it even when he was so upset. A smile she quickly banished when he looked up as he walked back toward her with the ridiculous stuffed animal.

Earl marched back to the car with the white and pink unicorn in one hand and Virgie in the other. Once she was settled and belted in, he started the car for home; she tried twice to talk but Earl silenced her with a look both times.

The minute he parked in her driveway she leapt from the car, grabbing her precious unicorn from the back. "I had a lovely time, Earl, but I think I'm kind of tired and..."

He snorted and grabbed her firmly by the arm to tow her into the house. "Nice try, little girl."

Inside he made short work of relieving Virgie of the unicorn and her pants and panties and seating himself on her couch. Then she was face down over his knee while his hand slapped down on her upturned bottom again and again.

Virgie jerked and yelped as he quickly built a fire in her nether regions that wouldn't soon be extinguished. Unfortunately every jolt brought her breasts closer and closer to breaking through their confines once more until they were swinging free in all their glory.

Earl flipped her up to straddle his thighs and took in the view. "I could get used to this here sweetheart neckline at home, Virgie girl," he told her as he leaned forward and sucked one pouting nipple deep into his mouth.

Virgie sighed and arched into him, her wet mound riding the fly of his jeans. "Earl, please!" she cried. "You know what it does to me to be taken in hand."

He obligingly reached between them, freed his aching cock from the confines of his jeans, and lifted her ass just enough for her to sink down on him, impaling herself.

They both cried out at the pleasure of their joining, Earl's hands coming up to cup her hot red bottom and guide her in a quick, hard rhythm as he continued to feast upon the bounty her bared breasts offered.

All too soon Virgie stiffened above him with a keening cry then began to shake in his arms with delicate convulsions as her inner muscles milked him dry. Earl groaned out his satisfaction into her neck, holding her close and kissing her gently.

"What do you want to do tomorrow, Earl?" Virgie asked with a mischievous sparkle in her eyes.

WHAT YOU NEED

Felicia smiled when she read the memo about a new program her company was instituting immediately, entitled *What You Need*. Her eyes zeroed in on the words *new snack machine in the employee lounge*.

She grinned and promptly dropped the memo into her trashcan. She already learned the most important thing; there was a snack machine in the lounge and she could get the Snickers bar she'd been craving all morning. Felicia studiously ignored the little extra jiggle in her hips that might indicate she didn't need a candy bar as much as she thought she did and made her way to the lounge.

A bright silver machine sat against the wall; it was the biggest snack machine she had ever seen and it didn't have any pictures or anything to indicate the selection. With a puzzled frown, she walked toward it.

At her approach a small flat panel slid out; directions were on it, instructing people to type their selection into the keyboard and then place their palm directly on the surface to the right.

"This is really weird," Felicia said aloud as she typed in 'Snickers bar' and then placed her palm flat on the indicated area. A whirring sound filled the air as brightly colored lights began to swirl beneath her palm.

She started when a mechanized voice sounded, "Felicia Summers, your selection does not compute with what you need; therefore, a more appropriate selection has been made for you."

"What?" she asked in surprise, and then glared when instead of the requested candy bar, a large red apple popped out of the slot instead. "Are you freaking kidding me? I want a Snickers, not an apple!"

"I must request you take your healthy snack and return to your desk or corporate compliance will be contacted," the machine said in its precise speech.

"I will not return to my desk. I want my Snickers bar, you big hunk of tin!" Felicia yelled and then gave the huge machine a little kick in frustration.

"What seems to be the problem here, young lady?" a firm male voice asked from directly behind her.

Felicia spun to face a very nice-looking older gentleman. Even though she was still very irritated, she couldn't help the spark of attraction that made all her girl parts pulse with anticipation.

"I ordered a Snickers bar and this stupid machine gave me an apple," she said with another glare at the machine.

"I see," the man said before walking up to the machine, punching a few keys, and collecting a little slip of paper that came out. "Hmmm, it says here that your body is dangerously low on fiber and other key nutrients needed to optimize your performance level and that a candy bar is not in your best interest at this time. It would be best if you took your apple like a good girl and returned to your desk. The machine has determined this is what you need."

Felicia was outraged. "I don't give a flying fig what the machine said! I want a Snickers bar and I refuse to eat that apple."

The machine gave another little whirring sound and then spit out a second slip of paper. The man collected the paper, read it, and then turned to Felicia with a look of resolve on his face. "Very well. I must insist you come with me, Ms. Summers."

"What? Why should I come with you? Who are you?" she asked, glaring up at the man who no longer seemed quite so attractive.

"My name is Abram Smythe; I'm the director of the new discipline division in corporate compliance. You're our first referral," he told her with a small smile while he began rolling up his shirtsleeves.

Felicia took a step back. "Discipline division? What exactly does that mean? Are you seriously going to write me up because I refused to eat an apple?"

"No, Ms. Summers. I have a much more effective way of dealing with noncompliance," Mr. Smythe said before catching her firmly by the upper arm and pulling her quickly down the hall into a door she'd never noticed before.

He stood her in the center of the room and got a straight-backed chair to sit in front of her, while Felicia watched him warily.

"Now, young lady, what do you have to say for yourself?" he asked from his position on the chair in front of her.

"About what?" she asked.

"Your refusal to do what's best for yourself," Mr. Smythe explained.

"Give me a break! I don't have to eat fruit if I don't like it! I'm well within my rights to have a candy bar!" she yelled down at him.

"You didn't read the memo this morning, did you?" he asked knowingly.

The man gave a sigh then pulled her face down over his lap, clamping his right leg over her thighs and lifting her skirt in almost one motion.

"What the hell are you doing!" she cried in alarm, finding herself unable to move from his iron grasp, then her panties were pulled down to the tops of her thighs, baring her to his gaze. "Hey!"

"If you'd bothered to read the memo, young lady, you would know your employers care about your health and what's good for you and have instilled some new policies accordingly. Failure to comply results in immediate disciplinary action; you will find if you read the fine print of your employment contract that the choice of discipline is at the discretion of your employer in any instances that it becomes necessary."

"But that doesn't mean you can…" She sputtered to a halt, unable to finish the sentence.

"Spank you? Yes, ma'am, it does," he said just before he brought his large palm down on her upturned posterior.

He followed the first slap with several in a row that left her howling and kicking her feet in vain as he began to deliver the worst spanking she'd ever received in short order.

Felicia lost count of how many times his hand fell as he spanked her, but the discomfort and heat in her poor bottom grew quickly.

By the time he stopped, her bottom felt like it could fire the furnace without any other heat sources and she was sure it was swollen to three times its normal size.

Mr. Smythe lifted her sobbing form to stand in front of him and turned her to face the corner. "Now you will spend some time in the corner reflecting on your behavior while I prepare your enema."

She spun to face him again in alarm. "Enema!" she screeched.

"Yes, you refused to eat the apple and afford your body of its fiber so the machine recommended an enema instead," he told her firmly. "I suggest you face the corner, young lady, or I will start your spanking again from the beginning."

Felicia spun to face the corner, all too aware her bright red bottom was on display to anyone who happened to walk in the door. He couldn't really give her an enema, could he? Surely this violated several labor laws. Her shoulders slumped… she really should have read the memo.

She wanted to protest the enema but the idea of repeating the spanking she'd already received on her hot sore backside wasn't something she could even bear to contemplate.

"I'm ready, Ms. Summers, drop your panties to the floor, raise your skirt to your waist, and bend over the end of the table." Mr. Smythe's instructions were very precise.

Felicia turned to see him standing there next to the table holding a thick, greasy-looking tube attached to a large bag hanging from an IV stand. She shuddered and began crying again as she shook her head at him.

"Now, Ms. Summers, it won't be as bad as you think, but if you don't comply with my instructions immediately I will add to the punishment you've already received."

"I just can't!" she cried.

"Very well, remember you made the choice. You will have a ginger plug to hold the enema after it's administered and then I will strap your bare bottom while your body absorbs the full effects of the enema and ginger plug. I assure you by the time it's all said and done, young lady, you will wish you'd bent over the end of the table as instructed." The implacable resolve made her bottom clench as she watched him attach the slick tube to the bag and come toward her.

Felicia turned to run but didn't even make it two steps before she was caught under his strong left arm, leaving her legs to windmill in the air. In a matter of seconds he'd pulled her panties free of her frantically kicking legs and unsnapped her skirt and pulled it from her body as well.

She was mortified to find herself completely bare from the waist down; to add insult to injury, his right hand began to bounce off her upturned bottom with each step he made toward the table.

"I'm sorry… I'll be good, I promise!" she cried as his hand fell again and again.

"Very well," he said as he set her down on her feet in

front of the table. "Bend over the end of the table and reach back and hold your bottom cheeks open for me."

She stared at him in horror, a little squeak the only sound that escaped her lips.

"Do you need further incentive?" he asked with a quirked brow.

Felicia practically threw herself over the end of the table and reached back to catch a burning bottom cheek in each hand as she spread herself wide open to his gaze with a shuddering sob. She'd never been so humiliated in her life; now a strange man was staring down at her tight little asshole, a sight no man had seen before, and he planned to stick that tube and a piece of ginger up it.

The little trickle of moisture escaping from her vaginal canal to line the lips of her labia only added to her mortification. What was wrong with her that she found this vile treatment arousing? She knew he could see everything from her cringing bottom hole to the moisture gathering below it. Were her lips swollen and wet?

"What a naughty little creature you are, Ms. Summers, something I would enjoy exploring another time, but today discipline is the only thing on the agenda. Naughty girls don't get to come. Remember that in the future, young lady."

She shivered at the subtle promise in his words. "Yes, sir."

Then she felt the press of the thick tube against her anus; he continued to press firmly against her little hole until it slid inside, stretching and burning the tight ring of muscle. When he had it all the way in, he patted her bottom lightly and then held it in place. She heard the snick as he released the valve and warm liquid began to flow into her bowels.

Felicia moaned as the fluid began to fill her to capacity. "Oh, no more, please!"

"Shhh, you've only received half the dose; once it's all in you'll have to hold it for ten minutes."

Her bowels were already protesting the intrusion and

cramping in response, but still it came until she felt her tummy swell as it was filled completely. Her anus contracted nervously as the tubing was removed, and then she felt something even thicker pressing against her sore little hole.

Mr. Smythe pushed the thick root in a little then twisted it before pulling it out again. He continued working it in and out of her bottom like a parody of anal sex until finally he pushed it all the way home. Felicia's bottom contracted around the thick root, squeezing it tightly and releasing its juices, making her whimper as the burn inside her ass grew.

"Ohh, it burns! Please… please take it out!" she cried.

"Next time you'll bend over the table the minute I ask, won't you, dear?" he asked, amusement apparent in his voice.

"Oh, yes, sir! I promise!" she cried fervently.

"I'm afraid you will have to hold it along with your enema for the entire ten minutes, my dear. Now I'm going to give you ten licks with the strap to finish your punishment."

"Nooo! Please…" she sobbed into the table.

"Release your bottom cheeks, young lady, I don't wish to injure your fingers," he instructed.

Felicia quickly brought her hands and arms to rest beneath her hot face, gasping when he did something to the table that lifted her feet from the floor and arched her bottom out prominently for punishment.

The first line of fire fell right in the crease where her bottom and thigh met, making her howl in pain. Mr. Smythe methodically striped her bottom from mid-thigh to just below where the end of the ginger root poked out from between her cheeks. Each stripe also served to jiggle the root and increase its burn inside her poor backside.

Felicia didn't even notice when the strapping ended; she just lay in place sobbing out her misery, her bottom burned inside and out and she knew she'd embarrass herself any minute.

A gentle hand stroked her lower back soothingly.

"There's my good girl. You took your punishment very well, Felicia; let me take this nasty root out and I'll help you to the bathroom."

Mr. Smythe pulled the burning root from her tender bottom then lifted her carefully to stand in front of him, hugging her to his side as he led her to the small toilet tucked behind a screen.

She was so eager to sit and release the enema, she didn't even try to get him to leave. Finally it was over and she even submitted to Mr. Smythe's help cleaning up. He was gentle now and caring; once she was all clean, he picked her up in his strong arms and carried her to a chair where he sat and cuddled her on his lap.

"You'll be my good girl from now on, won't you, Felicia?" he asked as he pressed a gentle kiss to her brow.

"Yes, sir," she promised softly, knowing she was forever changed.

"You were so good for me, I'm going to give you a little reward," he whispered in her ear as his long fingers slid between her thighs and found her slick heat.

Felicia groaned and spread her thighs wide for him; the hot burning in her ass and on her sore bottom cheeks suddenly made her ache to have him invade the only place he hadn't touched.

Three fingers shoved inside her aching sheath hard and fast as his thumb stroked her swollen clit in a circular motion. She came screaming and bucking in his arms a few seconds later.

"That was lovely, my dear. Let's have another," he said, sinking a finger from his other hand deep into her burning ass, stroking his fingers in and out of her in tandem while his thumb continued to ride her clit. Then he seemed to stroke the same spot high inside her from both sides until she began to shake as she built toward the strongest orgasm of her life. Felicia suddenly stiffened and her breath came out in a keening wail as she came hard, fluid spurting from her in the process until she lay spent in his arms.

"What a good girl you are," he praised her. "Would you like to have dinner after work?"

Felicia smiled. "I'd love to."

Later, after she was all cleaned up, dressed, and on her way back to her office, she saw a friend at the snack machine. Lisa was frowning down at the apple in her hand.

"Eat the apple!" Felicia yelled.

Lisa looked at her, startled by the outburst. "But..."

"Trust me, it's what you need."

THE BEAST

She waited, hiding in the shadows... a harsh guttural growl sounded from behind the house and her clit throbbed in response while her core clenched around nothing. He was looking for her, unhappy she wasn't waiting for him in the house.

Another fiercer cry sounded, the enraged sound of her husband in his more primal state looking for his mate.

A warm gush of arousal bathed her inner thighs; he would punish her for hiding when he found her and then he'd take her without mercy.

She almost moaned out loud at the thought.

Then she felt him behind her; she was caught but she still turned to run.

The effort was of course futile; he caught her long hair in his fist and pulled her up short. "Why are you hiding from me?"

She shivered. "I just wanted to play..."

The snort he gave in response was not one of amusement. "Oh, we will play, little mate, but it will be my game, not yours."

She whimpered when he pushed her to her knees, looking down at her as he shed his clothes until he was as naked as she. "All fours."

The command was barked with a snap, and she

immediately complied, arching her back for him and lifting her bottom high.

His hand landed hard and fast, moving quickly to paint her bottom a vivid red hue as tears dripped down her cheeks.

Then without warning her thighs were jerked wide and he thrust inside her brutally to the hilt; she gasped, grateful her wetness eased his entry, but still caught between pleasure and pain at the roughness of the joining.

A strong arm wrapped around her torso beneath her breasts and lifted her to her knees, her back against his chest, his big hand catching one breast and tweaking her nipple sharply.

She groaned and felt her inner muscles clamp down around his cock.

He growled against her neck and caught her tender flesh between his teeth in the spot where her neck joined her shoulder. His other hand snaked down her belly to possessively cup her mound.

He slipped nimbly between her wet lips and captured her clit, working it mercilessly as he began to move, taking her hard and fast.

She came with a scream, the suddenness of the climax taking her by surprise. Still he continued to pound in and out of her spasming sheath, releasing her to press her chest to the ground and hold her hips still.

He took her without mercy, slamming into her repeatedly until she came again with a harsh cry and he growled out his own climax, filling her with his seed.

In the aftermath he held her close, petting her gently as her breathing calmed. She turned in his arms to face him, touching his face with a smile.

"I love you, my beast."

A low rumbling growl was his only response.

THE END

STORMY NIGHT PUBLICATIONS WOULD LIKE TO THANK
YOU FOR YOUR INTEREST IN OUR BOOKS.

If you liked this book (or even if you didn't), we would
really appreciate you leaving a review on the site where you
purchased it. Reviews provide useful feedback for us and
for our authors, and this feedback (both positive comments
and constructive criticism) allows us to work even harder to
make sure we provide the content our customers want to
read.

If you would like to check out more books from Stormy
Night Publications, if you want to learn more about our
company, or if you would like to join our mailing list, please
visit our website at:

www.stormynightpublications.com

Made in the USA
Coppell, TX
26 July 2021

59530715R00069